Tilli's New World

Also by Linda Lehmann
BETTER THAN A PRINCESS

Tilli's New World

Linda Lehmann

ELSEVIER/NELSON BOOKS   New York

Copyright © 1981 by Linda Lehmann

Library of Congress Cataloging in Publication Data
Lehmann, Linda.
Tilli's new world.
Summary: Reunited with her immigrant family on a farm in Missouri, Tilli struggles against great odds to be allowed to go to school. Sequel to "Better than a Princess."
{1. Family life—Fiction. 2. Farm life—Missouri— Fiction} I. Title.
PZ7.L5324Ti 1981   {Fic}   81–5396
ISBN 0–525–66748–2   AACR2

Published in the United States by Elsevier-Dutton Publishing Co., Inc., 2 Park Avenue, New York, N.Y. 10016. Published simultaneously in Canada by Clarke, Irwin & Company Limited, Toronto and Vancouver
Editor Virginia Buckley   Designer Trish Parcell
Printed in the U.S.A.   First edition
10 9 8 7 6 5 4 3 2 1

*To the memory of my mother, Tilli,
who against great odds strove ever to learn
and rejoiced over each educational opportunity
granted her children*

Chapter 1

For the first few seconds after Tilli awoke, she lay tense with fear. Where was she? Still back with her foster family, the Baelks, in the Old Country? Had she only dreamed the long, long trip by immigrant ship and train and wagon to a place called Missouri?

Or had she actually reached her very own family at last and gone to sleep last night in their cabin loft, cuddling her new doll Lotti and listening to Father and Mother singing sweet-sad folk songs?

She sniffed. That tangy fragrance surely wasn't from the Baelk cow that used to be in a stall near Tilli's bed.

Tilli opened her eyes for a worried peek out from the warm featherbed. Almost directly above her, bunches of dried plants hung from rough roof logs. She felt around cautiously for the doll. Yes, the wonderful present from Mother was there!

Tingling with happiness, she held the doll close. It was all true, then!

For a time she dozed dreamily. Slowly another smell, very sweet, set her nose wrinkling in delight and her mouth watering. What could it come from? Something good to eat? Mmmmm! She took a deep, happy breath.

Father wasn't rich, she guessed, and Mother wasn't a princess, as Tilli had once imagined. But Tilli was here in her new world, in America, where everything wonderful would happen. She counted the best things off on her fingers. She'd surely never be hungry again, as she had always been in Europe. And now she'd have her own, real family. . . .

Suddenly she was aware of singing from below, different from that of last night. This was a lively and funny song, something about a thief discovered in a chicken house and pretending to be a rooster!

Tilli grinned sleepily, remembering how Adolf, on the ship, had called her brother Albert a rooster. Of course, Albert had some right to be cocky. He knew so much—all about kings and castles, and engines and numbers. He had gone to school. And now, marvel of marvels, she, too, would at last get to go, just as he had.

School! Suddenly Tilli jerked herself upright, the crisp straw inside her mattress crackling as she moved. She was breathing fast.

Had she overslept and missed school, this very first day home?

Sunlight was now bouncing upon the rough bark of the roof logs. Warmth was already seeping down to her. It must be late.

In Europe she herself had never been allowed to go. But she used to watch—oh, so enviously!—as children started down to the village school right after sunrise. Was it the same here? What if she was too late? Tilli's heart was pounding.

On the other side of the straw mattress her little sister Melia was still sound asleep. But the corner where Albert made his bed last night was empty. Was he off to school already, without her?

In a panic, Tilli hustled out from under the bulky featherbed and began slipping into her clothes. Maybe, if she hurried, she would still be in time.

Before she'd finished, a smile-y voice called from below. "Good morning, there! Are my two girls going to sleep their lives away? Better hurry down here! Breakfast's almost ready."

Mother! "Why, for a second I'd almost forgotten her!" Tilli confided to Lotti. Then she hugged herself in happiness. How special it was going to be, having a real mother! Everything would be all right from now on. And Mother wouldn't let her be late to school, surely.

In seconds after the call, Melia was up, too. Tilli hurried to help her dress. But it was Tilli who was first to clamber down the ladder.

Mother was busy stuffing split logs into the top of a black stove and quickly shoving back a lid before the flames could lick at her hands.

"We're here!" Tilli announced. "See? Are we in time?"

Mother turned around. She did not seem so tall as she had the night before. "*Ja, ja,* my girls, I see," she said. "*Ja,* in time. And hungry?"

Tilli hadn't meant in time for breakfast. She'd meant for school. But she was hungry! She nodded her head fast.

In between bobs, she glanced quickly at Mother. She didn't want to miss anything about her, yet didn't like to stare. Things looked very different with sunshine coming through the glass in the door from the way they had by lamplight last night. Now she saw that Mother's eyes were very blue—really blue-blue, not pale like "Mother"

3

Baelk's. And Mother's face was crinkled in a little smile, not a frown.

"Well, wash your faces, my girls," Mother directed, giving each a quick hug. "Over there's the basin, and the dipper and the roller towel." She pointed toward a rough bench. "We may have to start eating by ourselves if those men don't come in pretty soon. Your father must be showing that son of ours every rock and blade of grass on the place." She sounded proud and happy.

So Albert isn't at school yet, either, Tilli thought, and breathed more slowly.

She was puzzled by Mother's saying "those men." Why, Albert was only ten, barely two years older than she was!

Mother was waving toward the bench. Tilli still wondered about schooltime. "There'll be time yet left to get to school?" she asked hurriedly.

Mother's smile flattened out. Then she gave a quick laugh. "Oh, my, yes! Oceans of time. That's a long, long way off yet."

"Tomorrow?" Tilli asked. Surely it wouldn't be longer than that.

"My, my!" Mother laughed. "What a busy little question-box we have here this morning."

"But," Tilli persisted, "will it be tomorrow?"

"Oh," Mother sighed, "longer than that. Now to the washing."

Not tomorrow, Tilli told herself, but maybe the day after?

She skipped to the basin. When she cupped her hands into the water, it tingled her fingers. "It's cold!" she gasped.

"*Ja,* straight from our spring!" Mother said, her head high. "So lucky we are, not to need a cistern right away."

Tilli said, "Oh—" She didn't know what a spring or a cistern was, but she'd ask later. She helped Melia dab at eyes and cheeks. Soon they both were drying their faces on a part of the magical towel that rolled a clean, dry part down as they pulled it.

Mother was opening a door at the front of the stove and then lifting out a great black pan of something brown and crusty. It wasn't at all like the round loaves of dark bread people took out of the long, low brick oven in the village far away. And the fragrance was certainly the most wonderful Tilli had ever known!

She moved over to see better. "Oh! Oh! What is it?"

"Why, it's corn bread, my girl."

"Oooh! It looks so good!" Tilli clapped her hands.

"Well, let's hope you find it so," Mother drawled. "You will be seeing plenty of it this winter."

"The Mother and Father Baelk had mostly peas," Tilli said.

"Well, now, peas are very good—and good for you, *ja.* They make a fine soup."

"They didn't have soup from the peas." Tilli felt she must be completely truthful. "They just cooked them. They let me have those that fell in the sand on the floor."

Mother whirled around. "What do you mean—those in the sand?"

Tilli told her about the peas that "Father" Baelk had sometimes dropped on the sand-covered floor when he reached up for some of the cooked ones from a crock on the high shelf.

Mother's face grew sterner at every word.

"They didn't give you more than that? . . . and let you eat those from the floor?"

"But I wiped the sand off," Tilli protested. She must be fair, she thought. But it was good at last to be telling someone how it had been to be always hungry. "Then, sometimes I had barley gruel—by myself in the corner. I don't know what the others had at the table. Oh, and sometimes, too," she finished, "we all had mushrooms, lots of them. They were very good."

"Humph!" Mother sputtered. "Good, *ja,* but hardly enough to make a child grow strong."

She strode over and took Tilli by the shoulders while she looked her up and down. "You seem solid enough, my girl. It took more than mushrooms to do that."

"Oh, yes," Tilli began, "on the ship . . ." And then she told about the fine things Gus and Hans and Adolf the potato man had fed them while they traveled on the ocean.

"But"—Tilli giggled, pointing to Melia—"she didn't want any of the semmel rolls or the white bread. She wanted only black bread—*clebba,* she called it."

"*Clebba,*" Melia now repeated, coming closer.

Mother turned to her. "*Ja,* my girl, I know. Those Polish people call it *clebba.* And *clebba* with milk—now, that goes down fine, *ja?*"

Melia shook her head slowly. "No milk."

"No milk? Then what else?"

"Just *clebba,*" Melia insisted.

"I had no milk, either, where I was," Tilli added, moving near.

Mother scowled as though she didn't believe them at all.

"Why, your father told me those people had a cow. . . ."

Tilli felt she had to tell all of the truth. "Well, there was the cow, Spot. Mitzi and Sieg had milk."

"But not you—or you?" Mother's look shot from Tilli to Melia. They shook their heads.

Mother stared at them, while her face grew red. It was the way "Mother" Baelk's face had turned when she was about to whip Tilli. But Mother moved back to the stove, muttering something Tilli couldn't hear.

"And all the money we sent the *Herr Bürgermeister* for your keep!" she finished loudly. Then she began cutting the corn bread as though she were slicing off the mayor's head with each stroke.

"Well," she finally said, more quietly, "our Bossy won't have her calf till spring. But there's still some milk each day. We will see that you have milk while it lasts."

And right there she poured out two cups full to the brim and put them on the table. "Here," she said, "you might as well start. I see the men are coming at last."

Tilli sipped at her milk. It was cold and good. She put the cup down after a few swallows. She wanted it to last a long time.

In a moment the heavy door was pushed open. Albert and Father burst in, rubbing their hands and stamping their feet.

"The air really bites this morning," Father boomed. "See?" And he cupped Tilli's face in two chilly hands. She shivered, then giggled. His wavy mustache tickled when he kissed her cheek.

"And how are the sleepyheads?" he continued, grabbing Tilli under her arms and swinging her up so high her hair brushed the cross logs of the ceiling. Oooh! It was fun!

He didn't give her time to catch enough breath to answer before he did the same to Melia.

Meanwhile Albert was bouncing up and down in excitement. "Tilli! Melia!" he exclaimed. "You must see them! There are golden fish in the creek!"

Gold, thought Tilli—golden fish! Then Mother and Father must be rich, after all!

"Where? Real gold? Where, Albert?"

"Right down there," he said, starting to point. Tilli could see he wasn't sure which way to show her. "Somewhere out there," he finished.

Tilli started for the door. "I want to see!"

"Not so fast, my buzzing bee!" warned Mother. "Breakfast first. And not so loud. You will be waking Victor."

Victor?—The baby, of course! My baby brother, thought Tilli. How could one remember about so many things at once?

"Is he any better, you think, Vina?" Father asked in a very subdued voice.

Mother shook her head slowly. She looked down. Her mouth made only a thin line.

What was wrong? Tilli wondered. "Where is he?"

Mother nodded toward an inside door. "But not now!" she ordered when Tilli started in that direction. "Now the corn bread."

At the very first bite, Tilli forgot about Victor, about the golden fish, even about school. The corn bread was warm and crumbly, and it tasted—oh, it tasted so good, she wanted more and more!

"Here," Father urged her, "dip yours in the molasses,

like this." He passed a dish and showed how to dunk the corn bread into a thick brown syrup.

"Oooh! Oooh!" Tilli exclaimed between sticky bites. She dipped again and again.

"If she doesn't want the flies to carry her off," Mother finally said, "I think one little girl had better stop eating molasses. Besides, that jug over there is for the whole winter."

When everyone had finished, Albert announced, "Now then, the fish!"

"Now the dishes," corrected Mother. "Surely I have at least one girl big enough to help me." She looked directly at Tilli. *"Ja?"*

"Oh, yes," Tilli admitted. It would be lots different, helping Mother, from being shouted at by the Baelks. But she hoped the golden fish would still be there when she was through

At last the table was cleared, the dishes washed, rinsed, and dried. Tilli was slow with her part of the work because she studied the blue flowers on each dish as she wiped.

"Now the golden fish?" Tilli looked to Mother for permission.

Mother nodded. "But first we take off those good shoes. It should be warm enough by now. And the shoes have to last."

"Come now, sisters!" Albert urged them when they were barefooted.

All three hurried outside.

Tilli found the ground still cold. Her feet had been in real shoes most of the time since leaving the far-off village. Now she felt prickles as she hopped over the pebbles and the dried grasses. But her eyes were taking in all the things missed the night before. There was so much to see! The potato patch where she'd stumbled in the half-dark seemed much smaller now. The cabin looked warm and brown, not black.

Albert pointed out the log shed where the livery-stable horses and the cow were. My, it was so much closer to the cabin than it had seemed in the dim twilight.

"Yes, yes," Tilli said. "But the golden fish—?"

"Right back of this rock," Albert assured her. He stalked ahead to show the way, then pointed to a huge flat rock. It was as big as half the cabin loft.

"Look!" Albert was motioning excitedly. "It'll be a fortress where we can play soldiers and have battles."

"No, no," Tilli protested. "It'll be a ship. See, we could—"

She didn't finish for, just beyond, the ground sloped down sharply to a pool of clear water. "Oh, oh!" she shouted.

"Right there!" said Albert. "See them? There are the golden fish!"

Sure enough! Tilli saw them gliding around the edge of the water—beautiful, gold-colored fish! Most were longer than her hand. They slipped past one another so smoothly! They were wonderful.

"I want to feel them!" Tilli cried.

"Me, too!" said Melia.

"You can't," Albert warned. "I already tried. They won't let you."

Tilli had to be sure, though. She reached down to the water, nearly tumbling in. The nearest fish flipped around and looped away.

10

"See?" said Albert.

Melia was already squirming down to the edge of the pool. "I want to feel," she said and dipped in one bare foot. She jerked it out at once. "Ooooh!" she squealed. "It's too cold!"

Tilli knew she could be braver. She put one foot in. She shivered and caught her breath. The cold stung her toes and sent a shudder through her. But she kept them under.

In a moment one of the fish swam close and began nibbling at her big toe. Tilli was so surprised she jerked her foot out. "It tickles!" she giggled.

Melia tried putting her toes in again. Several fish slid over to investigate. "They try to bite me!" she complained. But she was grinning happily.

Then Tilli put both feet in. More fish swam up to her toes.

Albert, too, was dipping his feet down to the inquisitive fish.

Such laughing, such fun Tilli couldn't ever remember.

Oh, it was going to be more wonderful at home than she'd even imagined! To have fun like this, to have lots of food . . . so good! And her own family . . .

Only one thing troubled her. When would she start school? How long was that "long, long way off" Mother had mentioned? Tomorrow? Or not till the day after?

Chapter 2

Tomorrow arrived, then other tomorrows, and Tilli wondered. There was no more mention of school.

Each morning, however, brought some new discovery, excitement, or surprise. And it was one of these that particularly sent Tilli's spirits bouncing sky-high.

"I have to return the horses and wagon," Father announced early that day. "I'll be picking up the new horse I'm buying, and a cart. Who wants to go along with me to Sedalia?"

And school, Tilli hoped secretly. It must be in Sedalia.

All three children shouted, "I do!" But Tilli was first.

"Well," said Father, "from the way I remember it, there'll be room in that cart for only one besides me—and of course my boy here." Father clapped Albert on the shoulder. "That is, if he can ride the new horse," he added.

Tilli watched Albert puff himself up. "Yes, of course!" he boasted. "I often got to ride one of the carriage horses back in Dienbau."

"That's my boy!" Father exclaimed. "Now then—" His eyes zigzagged from Tilli to Melia. "Who else?"

Tilli's heart was thumping so loudly, she was sure Father

could hear it begging for her. Mother signaled something to him.

Then he said, "Well, Tilli, my girl, get your shawl."

The ride was long, but it seemed shorter than it had that first trip out to the farm. When they reached town, they passed many, many houses lined up neatly along the streets. Tilli kept looking at them, astonished. They were all different—and so big!

At last the wagon was approaching a wide, open space. There lots of children were shouting and racing as they played some game. Tilli guessed right away what the nearby brick building might be, and her heart almost stopped.

"Look, see!" she urged, tugging at Father's sleeve. "A school, isn't it?"

Father turned to look. "*Ja, ja,* a school, of course," he answered without enthusiasm.

"And we're going there—now?" Tilli's words tumbled together.

"What for?" Father asked. "We are going to the livery stable."

"But then, after that? Is this where I go to school?"

Albert, too, asked quickly, "Will we, Father?"

Tilli was holding very still, not to miss his reply. But it took another "Will we, Father?" before that came.

"Now, how would you two get here every day, just tell me! Surely you can see it's much too far to walk." He thought for a short while, then chuckled. "Why, it'd take so long, you'd be bumping into yourself as you met yourself coming and going."

Tilli tried to picture how she could meet herself. It didn't seem funny at all. She felt as if she had swallowed a stone.

13

"But," she tried again, "if we're getting a horse of our own—"

"Yes," Albert broke in eagerly, "I could ride—"

Father didn't answer him. He turned to Tilli instead. "A horse," he explained to her, "would be for working the fields, *Mädchen,* not for trotting back and forth to school—see? And, thunder and lightning, why would a horse want to go to school, anyway?" Again Father laughed.

Tilli couldn't say anything. She felt choked up. Father gave her a searching stare. "My, my!" he exclaimed. "Why such a cloudy face?"

Tilli sniffed and swallowed hard.

"Disappointed, little one?" he said in a kindly tone.

Tilli nodded.

"Well, my girl," Father went on, cradling her shoulders awkwardly, "maybe when we harvest the corn, there'll be enough to sell some and buy at least a schoolbook for you. How would that be?"

Tilli thought about that a moment. At first she was excitedly happy, but soon the pleasure drained away. A book would be ever so nice to have. But what good would one be to her, when she couldn't read?

Albert, though, was jubilant. "Oh, I'd like that very much!" he said. "And then, too, I might read to you all!"

That could help some, Tilli imagined. But it didn't cheer her much on the jouncy ride home in the cart. When they again passed the school, the playground was empty. They're all inside learning, Tilli told herself. How she envied them. The farther she got away, the worse she felt. She tried to imagine walking all the miles the new horse trotted, and she decided Father must be right.

When they were back home, Melia wanted to know all

about the trip. Tilli did her best in telling. "And I saw the school! But we didn't go in. We didn't even stop," she ended with a sigh.

"*I* rocked little Victor," Melia said proudly. "And I helped Mother find nuts! And I'm learning to count with them!"

Tilli didn't listen very carefully. What were nuts, anyway, compared to school?

But by the next morning, she was as eager as the others as they went out to gather more. There were hickory nuts and walnuts and pecans under the trees, and hazel nuts in the brush along a crooked rail fence. Why, it was like finding free treasures! The gathering soon turned into busy contests to see who could find the most.

Better still, that evening Mother used some of the nuts to teach both girls counting in English. Tilli was more enthusiastic even than Melia had been.

"See here," Mother said, pushing a fat pecan shell to the side, "*eins*—one. Say it."

"One," the girls chimed back.

Mother pushed another nut over. "*Zwei*—two."

"Two."

"*Drei*—three."

"Three!" Tilli and Melia almost shouted. My, it was fun!

So it went all the way through *zehn*—ten. Then Mother went over the ten numbers several more times.

Finally she said, "That's enough for now. Let's see how much you remember." She shoved one nut at a time into a heap and after each move asked for the name of the total.

"One—*zw*—no, two—" Of course even Tilli stumbled some, but she promised herself she'd learn them all soon.

She thought that already she was sure of the names through six.

Next Mother put the questions in a different way. She had seven nuts together, then pushed three away.

"How many are left?—Melia?"

Melia looked puzzled. "*Sechs*—six?" she ventured.

Mother shook her head solemnly. "Tilli?"

Tilli had been counting carefully. "*Vier!*" she said triumphantly.

"English!" Mother said it almost fiercely.

Tilli started over. "F—f—" Oh, what was the English word?

Mother had to help out. "Four. One, two, three, four. Now try to remember them all. Another time we'll learn more. One should surely know how to count before going to school."

Tilli put herself to sleep that night trying to recite the English names for those numbers, all the way to ten. She must do all she could to get ready for school, whenever that would be.

She practiced counting, too, as the nuts were husked out of their rough coats, or, better still, were cracked open on the sadirons with a hammer, so that the meaty parts could fall out. "*Elf*—no, e-leven! twelve, thirteen . . ."

Sometimes Tilli would lose count as she studied the strange irons. They were heavy, pointed ones, with bowed handles, not at all like the Baelk iron that slipped into a shiny brass holder. It was more interesting, though, to watch Mother get ready to iron with these. She put them on the hottest part of the stove top. Then, when she wanted to use them, she made a holder out of folded paper or cloth for lifting an iron to test its heat. She held the iron with one hand and wet the fingertips of the other with her tongue, then quickly touched the bottom of the iron with those fingers. If there was a little sizzle, Tilli learned, Mother knew the iron was hot enough to use for pressing.

"Could I try it?" Tilli begged. It looked really exciting.

"And burn one of your fingers?" Mother answered. "Or drop it on your toes? It could mash them as easy as a hammer does nutmeats when one isn't careful."

Of course the irons were cold when Tilli and Albert cracked the nuts. Tilli's first efforts were so clumsy! With the iron lying on its side, the round, hard nuts would fly off as she came down with the hammer and hit only the iron with a loud clang. Or she'd hit so hard, all the nutmeats would be smashed, as Mother had said, and be mixed in with the mouth-puckering shells. And once, when Tilli was holding a particularly slippery nut, she hit her thumb instead. Oh, how that hurt! She could feel the hot pain clear to her stomach.

But when things went right, there were little pieces of the sweet, rich nutmeats to nibble. Tilli took very little bites to make each last longer. All the big pieces went into the brown crockery jar for winter use.

"They will taste even better in *Kuchen*," Mother promised.

Tilli wondered how anything could taste better than the bits of pecans or hickory nuts or the very-hard-to-crack black walnuts, unless it was the warm, foamy milk Mother sometimes gave her in her special little blue cup as she watched the milking.

It was magical the way Mother's hands worked at Bossy's

udder and the streams of milk went swishing into the pail.

"Couldn't I try?" Tilli asked one morning. She could hardly keep from reaching over right then.

Mother turned her head for an odd look at Tilli. "That chance will come soon enough when you are older, I can tell you." She laughed.

"But couldn't I now?"

"What a girl!" Mother chuckled as if telling Bossy a joke.

"Please?"

Mother paused in her milking. "Well," she began slowly, "if you'll get that smaller pail from the table so we can pour this safely into it first. There's not enough milk these days to waste any."

Tilli was off and back with the little pail before Mother could change her mind.

"Now," said Mother, when the milk was transferred and the big pail ready for Tilli to use, "sit here like this. . . ."

Tilli slipped onto the stool beside Bossy. She felt the cow's warmth as she bent close the way Mother did. Bossy turned her head as if to see what was happening.

"Now then," Mother directed, "wrap your hand around one teat like this, then squeeze."

Tilli found that her fingers wouldn't reach all around. Then she tried using both hands. She squeezed hard. No milk came. Bossy shifted her weight uneasily.

"Oh, oh!" Mother explained. "You're squeezing up, and that hurts Bossy. I should have told you first: you must squeeze from the top down, one finger at a time, like this." And she demonstrated in the air.

This time Tilli got some milk to come out, a tiny streak. She tried again and again. She was so excited! "It works!" she cried.

Sometimes it didn't, though, because she forgot about one finger at a time. Bossy would give a quiet, troubled moo. Once the milk squirted clear out of the pail. Then Mother warned Tilli, "Careful! The straw doesn't need any breakfast!"

Soon Tilli's fingers were so tired they felt numb. "I guess that's all I can do right now," she confessed with a sigh.

Mother agreed and sat down to finish.

"But can't I do it again—soon?" Tilli asked.

Mother nodded as she stripped out the last drops and stood up.

Tilli raced out of the shed to find Albert. "I'm learning to milk!" she shouted as soon as she saw him. "Mother let me, just now!"

Tilli thought that for a moment he looked envious. But then he tossed back his head. "Well, well," he said, looking down at her, "that's not much to be proud about."

He surely looked like a strutting rooster now, Tilli thought. But her cheeks grew hot.

"Well, can *you* milk?" she asked as haughtily as she could.

"Of course not! That's girls' and women's work!"

"Well, well—" Tilli didn't know how to go on. But then she flashed out at him. "What things can you do?"

"Oh, lots of things, just lots of things already! Father lets me help hitch up the new horse. You know that very well."

Tilli did know that, of course. Hadn't she watched impatiently, wishing she had that chance, as he struggled clumsily with the harness?

"And," Albert went on, "he's going to show me how to plow, and to cut wood."

Tilli felt her bubbles of excitement being pricked flat.

But just the same, she drew herself up. "And—?" she asked, just as if Albert had said nothing important at all.

"Well," he began, "that's a mighty lot already. And if you must know, this afternoon we're going to shuck some of the corn."

"What's that, shucking corn?"

"You don't know that!" Albert sounded as astonished as if Tilli had said she didn't know her own name. "Why—you shuck, or husk the corn," he said, "so we can get more meal ground for corn bread, or corn to sell."

Tilli thought of the half-promised schoolbook. Her interest perked up. "But what do you do when you husk the corn?" she wanted to know.

"Oh,"—Albert shrugged—"you just husk it, that's what." He began to stride off. "Make Father tell you, silly, if you don't know."

Why, he doesn't really know himself! Tilli thought.

At noon she didn't ask Father what husking was. What she did ask was to help.

Mother turned to Father. Tilli saw her wink. "We have an eager little elf here, it seems. Better let her try."

"Sure, sure," Father agreed. "Many hands will make the husks fly."

"Me, too!" Melia begged. "I want to see them fly."

"Not yet," Mother corrected her. "You and I will watch Victor to see he doesn't get to choking again. Besides, husking corn isn't easy. I doubt your big sister will last very long out there, anyway."

Tilli was sure she'd prove Mother wrong. "And I'll be helping to get the money for that schoolbook," Tilli thought happily.

Chapter 3

At the first tall, tentlike shock of corn, Father cut with a loud pop through the twine holding the stalks together. Then he reached for one of the dry ears and broke it loose.

His eyes were twinkling as he juggled the ear in one hand.

"Good! Full!" He smiled broadly and began stripping off the dry covering. "Watch now. We husk like this."

Tilli kept her eyes busy as he separated the crinkly dry silks that hung from the top, then pulled them and the husks down. Out popped most of a golden ear with its even rows of kernels. It looked easy to do.

"Fine corn!" Father exclaimed and turned to survey the lines of other shocks in the field. "I got a mighty lucky buy, after all—this farm and the harvest all in!" His chest rose as he stood for a moment to enjoy the prospect. Then he flailed his arms as though shooing chickens.

"Well now, to work! Each of you throw the shucked ears on a pile of his own. We'll soon see who works fastest."

Tilli promised herself she would be the one—well, not faster than Father, probably, but surely, than Albert.

She searched for another fat ear on the shock. Here was one! She tried to break it off as Father had done with his, but it took several hard tugs and twistings with both hands before it came free. And then she went sprawling backward.

Albert snickered as she hurried to pick herself up, "See!" He had already snapped an ear off, stripped it down, and broken the ear out, to begin his pile.

"Well, I did get it loose!" Tilli muttered, but not loudly enough for him to hear. Then she struggled to clear away the husks from the ear she held. When she had most of them peeled down, she tugged and tugged to break the stem from the base of the husks. But it wouldn't snap off. She looked at Father, who was tossing down his third or fourth ear.

"It works even better if you just leave the ears on the stalk, I think," he told the children. Then he laughed apologetically. "Well, I have to find out the best way myself. I hear the farmers in this country even have races to see who first can finish shucking out a whole shock of corn."

He glanced at Tilli, then chuckled. "So, little one," he said, half smiling at her efforts, "giving up already?"

Tilli tried harder. "Oh, no! No! It's just—it's just that this won't break off!"

"I told her she couldn't do this kind of work," said Albert loftily. "I told her it was really man's work."

"Hold on, there, my young grasshopper!" Father scolded. "You should have seen your mother when we did that first shock, the one that was closest to the cabin. She snapped the ears out like the popcorn flying out of that machine in town. And if it weren't for the sick baby, she'd be out here beating us all, I'm ready to swear! Here," he directed Tilli, "I'll break that for you. From now on, just get yours stripped down that far. I'll do the rest for you."

"But she can't win that way!" Albert protested.

Tilli sighed. It was bad to lose before she'd really begun. And she had so wanted to help get lots of corn ready to sell! But after she tried again several times, she slowly handed her ear over to Father.

Before long, even just stripping away the husks was roughening her fingers and making her whole hands sting.

Father was piling up all the stalks from which the ears had been husked. Tilli and Albert waited for him to reach a new layer of corn-heavy stalks. Father went all around the shock, feeling with one hand.

"What's this?" he grumbled and began pulling away stalk after stalk and tossing it to the ground. As far as Tilli could tell, no heavy ears hung from any of them. Father moved faster and faster.

"Thunder and lightning!" he shouted. "What poor corn that man raised!"

Father kept stripping away more empty stalks, until the shock itself was getting thin, like a once fat, melting icicle.

Suddenly he stopped, stared at the few stalks that had been tied together to make the center of the shock. Then he hurled out without stopping a string of wild words that made Tilli cringe. In between the peppery language she understood some fearful things. "Shucked out! . . . Not a tenth of what I paid for! . . . All the inside corn gone! . . . Such a double-blasted villain!"

All the while, Father was tearing apart what was left of the shock and what he had thrown on the ground. He kept feeling for any ears he might have missed. But there were only barren stalks, empty husks where the corn had already been ripped out.

What would this mean? Tilli's fear grew. Wouldn't there be any corn left to sell? The whole shock was leveled. And the only grain from it turned out to be her six ears, Albert's few, and Father's little heap—all from just the outside stalks.

Father was now shaking his head, puzzled. "But the rascal showed me how much corn there was!" Father seemed to be arguing with Albert and Tilli. "And that first one over there gave us two bushel baskets full."

Suddenly his face brightened. "Well, now," he began with a relieved sigh, "this has to be a mistake. He probably forgot he'd started to collect the harvest here before he sold me the land."

Tilli breathed easily again.

Father walked briskly to the next shock, snapped the twine, and hurriedly threw down the outer stalks with their full ears dangling from them.

"There, you two, get busy with those." He snatched away several other stalks. They proved to be bare. Then, with furious speed, he threw stalks away in all directions until he got to the very center of that shock.

Without a word he strode to another and did as before. Again Tilli's fears grew as she saw him break out full ears on the outer layer of the shock, or throw those full stalks down, then find no corn on the inside stalks.

When he got down to the core of the fourth shock, he let out an explosion of frightening words that chilled Tilli worse than a splash of the spring water on her face.

" 'Dumb Dutchman,' they call me," he sputtered at last. "And dumb Dutchman that villain has made me! Now what will we have to eat this winter? The cow has these stalks, the pig can fill up on acorns, but we—" He didn't finish.

Tilli shuddered. Father was shouting again, but now he

seemed afraid, not just angry. And that made Tilli afraid, too. Nothing to eat! She still remembered too well the hollow feeling every day at the Baelks' house. And now to that empty feeling was added the disappointment that seized her at the thought that, with no corn to sell, there surely couldn't be any money for that schoolbook.

After that day Tilli noticed how at each breakfast the corn bread seemed thinner and the molasses Mother set out in the dish less and less. No one complained, though, least of all Tilli. How could she dare say anything that might start Father sputtering in anger or in shame again? Having that schoolbook seemed more desirable the smaller the chances of getting it. Yet what was her disappointment compared to everyone's being hungry? What if Father's fears came true?

He didn't really seem discouraged. He and Albert went out often to try hooking catfish from the creek.

"Not the golden fish?" Tilli asked in alarm at first. What if their "pets" were to be caught—and eaten?

"Those?" Father almost spat out the word. "Carp? Those scavengers! They don't make good eating."

"Beggars can hardly be choosy," Mother was quick to remind him.

The "men" were more likely to be successful in hunting rabbits or squirrels. And when they were, it was a very extraordinary day. For supper Mother would have a stew that set Tilli's lips smacking.

One special afternoon Mother surprised the girls with a toy animal. She had made it from the skin of one of the squirrels. She had dried and stuffed it so that it looked fat and perky.

What fun it was for Tilli and Melia to toss it from one to

the other and see the tail streak behind it! It seemed just like the real squirrels they sometimes saw running under and up the oak trees on the hill.

"It's so real!" said Melia. "It looks alive."

That's when Tilli got her idea. "Yes, just like a live one!" She could hardly keep her excitement from boiling over. "Melia," she confided in a very hushed voice, "we could play a joke on Albert with it."

"How?"

"Just put it up on that branch there to make believe it's eating an acorn. Then we'll tell Albert to look and see. And we'll fool him, we will! He's the one Father always thinks is so smart. We'll show him!"

Melia popped up. "Let me do it!" she begged. "I can climb better."

She scrambled up on the first branch, then called down, "Quick, Tilli! Reach it to me."

Tilli did. Melia put the toy squirrel on the limb above her, right against the trunk. "I've got it fixed now!" she squealed.

Tilli looked up to see. The squirrel didn't seem quite right. "Try to put the tail over its head," she directed. "Now move its front paws up to the mouth. That's the way. Oh, now it looks really real, Melia! Come down and see."

They were both so pleased with themselves, they could hardly hold back their grins when they saw Albert trudging home with Father. Tilli could see that they hadn't shot any game this trip.

"Look, Albert, a squirrel!" Melia called, pointing to the toy.

Albert took a quick look in its direction, then rushed back to Father. Tilli heard him reporting excitedly,

"There's one right there, Father! Can't I try to get it?"

Father must have agreed. Albert was back in a sputter of directions: "Get back near the cabin, Melia! Tilli! And hurry! Father's going to let me shoot it. Out of the way!"

He lifted Father's gun and aimed.

Before there was any loud report, however, a sudden breeze caught the squirrel, and it tumbled to the ground.

"I got it! I got it! Did you see?" Albert was so excited he dropped the gun and ran for the squirrel.

Tilli motioned for Melia to come close. Both girls were trying to cover grins with their cupped hands. Then, as Albert reached for the toy, the girls shrieked, "Fooled you! Fooled you!" They were clapping and jumping up and down. "Fooled you, we did!"

Albert was squeezing the squirrel carefully and staring at it, perplexed. "Aw, you!" he finally grumbled. "It's not a real squirrel at all."

"No," Melia squealed, "we fooled you, I tell you!"

Albert still looked puzzled. "But I shot it. It fell."

"Naw, naw!" Father chuckled as he picked up the gun. "You don't think I'd let a young hothead like you have my gun without first taking out the shot, do you?"

He moved closer. "Now, let's have a look at your 'squirrel.' Well, well! I bet I don't have to guess twice about who fixed this—your mother, wasn't it?" His heavy eyebrows lowered. He looked almost accusingly at the girls.

"Yes, yes." They nodded.

"And what little mischief put it up in the tree like that?" Father sounded very stern. Melia moved to hide behind Tilli.

"You, Amelia?" Father seemed even more severe.

Melia didn't answer.

Tilli felt her chest getting hot. She knew she couldn't let Father believe the wrong thing any longer. "Melia put it up there," she said in a tiny voice, "but—I told her to."

Tilli expected a spanking right there. But instead Father slapped a hand on her shoulder and roared. "Well, well, that's my Tilli! I can count on her. She always tells the truth."

Tilli took a very deep breath.

"And now," Father went on, "we'd better get inside and see whether that clever mother of yours can make nothing into a meal that looks and tastes real. Because that's exactly what we brought home—nothing."

Tilli was worried. But he swept the squirrel toy up for a close look. As he headed for the cabin, he began laughing till the hills answered him back.

Chapter 4

But there were things that followed that Father couldn't laugh away.

Only once in a while did Mother let the girls carry little Victor or rock him in his hollowed-log cradle. He wasn't lively like the Baelk children. Mostly he just lay still or whimpered. When Tilli felt his face, it was hot but not baby pink. She couldn't understand. He didn't seem to be aware of those around him. Seeing him so listless made Tilli fearful. What was the matter?

Finally there was the night when she woke up suddenly. Right off she sensed that something was very wrong. Everything should have been dark and quiet. Instead a light was still burning down below. Its strong coal-oil smell was thick in the loft.

Very carefully Tilli rolled over on her mattress far enough to see. Mother was pacing the floor. Her hair was hanging loose over her nightgown, and she was cradling a very quiet Victor in her arms. It sounded as if she were praying. Then Tilli almost gasped. She saw tears rolling down Mother's cheeks. They glinted in the lamplight.

Those tears frightened Tilli most of all. She had never seen Mother cry. What terrible, terrible thing was happening?

Tilli hardly dared breathe. After a very long time she thought she heard Father asking something. She strained to see Mother bend her head closer over Victor, then look away and shake her head slowly. Tilli couldn't see her face, but she heard a deep sob as Mother moved out of sight.

Tilli inched back on her mattress. She reached for Lotti. It helped smooth away the heavy lump in her throat to feel the doll's curls cuddled against her. But she lay stiff and still till at last she went back to sleep.

In the morning when she crept down the ladder, she found Mother alone. It was so strange not to hear her singing that Tilli waited a long while before asking, "Where's Albert?—and Father?"

Mother's voice sounded gruff as she answered, her back still to Tilli. "They have work to do outside."

Tilli listened. She thought she heard hammering.

"Are they making something?"

Mother didn't answer.

Tilli wondered whether her silence had anything to do with last night. She had to know about Victor! She began tiptoeing toward the bedroom door.

"No, Tilli, no!" Mother's voice was low but sharp. "You don't want to go in there now. Stay away from there!"

Then Tilli guessed she knew why. A chill stiffened her, and tears came to her eyes.

"Victor—is he—" It was hard to get the words out. "Is he with the dear Lord?"

Mother nodded slowly. Tilli stumbled over to her, clutching the gray apron to her own eyes.

Mother reached down to push the hair from Tilli's cheek. Then she bent to stare at Tilli through reddened eyes. "*Ja, ja, Mädchen,*" she said tenderly. "But how could you know such a thing?"

"That other time," Tilli began. A memory from some faraway place and time was flooding over her again, as it had once on the ship. "There was a baby—I think it was a baby—" she recalled, "being carried in a white box, on a man's shoulder. . . . And people were singing and walking in a line along a road . . . between picket fences."

It all seemed very vividly real to Tilli even now. "The people all sat down. . . . There was a hill there. And an old man stood up and said the baby was with the dear Lord. Some people were crying when the box went in the ground. But some kept saying, 'He is with the dear Lord.' "

"It was a beautiful hope." Mother sighed and wiped her eyes. She was silent for a while, then turned abruptly to Tilli again. "You remember all that?"

Tilli nodded. But to be surely truthful, she said, "I think so. . . ."

"How could you?" Mother said, more to herself than to Tilli. Her hand was on Tilli's shoulder. "To think you could remember all that! Why, when your other little brother died, you weren't more than a baby yourself. Let's see now—you weren't even four!"

Tilli was puzzled. "That was my brother, too?"

"*Ja, ja.*" Mother sighed again.

Another half-memory was troubling Tilli. "Was that the box that was all white inside, too?—with a paper pillow, and blanket all so real—and a beautiful white, shiny angel inside the lid?"

The picture memory was awesome but somehow wonderful.

Mother drew Tilli closer. "*Ja,* it was such a box—white, and lacy inside." She pressed Tilli's shoulder.

In spite of that comfort, Tilli suddenly shivered. She remembered something else. She reached an arm up to half encircle Mother's waist.

"Mother," she asked slowly, "was a man there—a man who started to lay someone in the box—and said it was such a nice little bed?" Even now she shuddered, reliving the horror she'd felt then.

Mother grew stern. "Yes, my girl, that's true. That man, your father! The things he can sometimes make light of!"

She released her arm and shrugged, then became brusque once more. "Set the table, my girl. The men will be wanting something to eat after their work."

And so it was that another brother was laid into a box, this one very crude and rough, with no paper satin pillow or beautiful angel on the lid. He was put into the ground, and Father built a plain log fence around the place to keep the pig and any foxes away.

For a long time after that, Tilli thought neither she nor anyone else in the family could ever laugh or be happy again. She pushed aside her feeling of disappointment about school or a schoolbook. How could she feel sorry about them when ever so much sadder things had happened? If only Victor were back and her family could be glad together again!

During those gloomy days Mother hardly said a word. Meals were very solemn. Worst of all, nobody ever sang.

But after what seemed to Tilli like forever, there came a morning when things suddenly changed. To her it was like breaking out into the open after being in one of the big dark holes by the creek. She had tiptoed in from outdoors to get warm, and she found Mother humming a tune.

She even had a half-smile on her face as she turned to Tilli. "Did you know, my girl," she asked, teasingly, "that you have a birthday tomorrow?"

"A birthday?" Tilli couldn't help clapping her hands. "Will I be nine then?"

"Not so fast! You will be eight, *Mädchen.*"

"Eight?" Tilli was all mixed up. The "Mother" Baelk had often said a girl in her eighth year was big enough for all kinds of work. "Only eight?" Tilli persisted. "Not nine?"

"Just eight," Mother said, then continued with a quick laugh, "I guess I ought to know when you were born! Didn't we have to break the ice in the water pail for your first bath? I couldn't forget that, could I?"

Tilli shivered. "Oooh!"

"Well," said Mother, "I don't think it will be that cold tomorrow in this country, so you needn't trouble your little head about that. And did you know that'll be Saint Nicholas' Day, too?"

Tilli was puzzled. "Saint—what did you say?"

"Saint Nicholas. But this time there won't be any man in a brown-checked suit pretending to be the saint, and scaring you half to death."

Tilli couldn't figure out what Mother was talking about. "Scaring me? Saint Nicholas? Who is that?"

"Why, he's a good saint who, they say, comes every year on the sixth of December to help people prepare for the Christ Child's own birthday. The dear Lord's—"

"Then why would he scare—" Tilli broke in, but didn't

finish. For a flicker of time she thought she remembered a fierce man in a brown-checked suit. But she wasn't really sure. It was easy to imagine things.

"Oh, the saint or one of his helpers," Mother explained, "tries to visit all the children to see whether they've been good and know their prayers. If so, well, then he leaves them some nice sweets in the shoes they put out for him. But if they've been bad, he may leave a switch instead."

Tilli cringed.

"But this man!" Mother continued without noticing. "Oh, he and your father were always up to some nonsense together! One year he came pretending he was Saint Nicholas—on your birthday, of course. I guess it was when you were three. He had his hair and beard combed crazily, as if a whirlwind had done it. And he wore an ugly, ragged black cape over that checked suit he always had on."

Whether she was remembering or only imagining, Tilli wasn't sure. But Mother's vivid telling was sending chills along Tilli's arms.

"He came right up to you children, shouting angrily for your prayers. Not to Albert, of course. He knew who the man was. But you and Melia screamed as if you'd seen a werewolf. Well, I tell you, I had to take you both and hide you in the featherbed until he was gone."

Tilli wondered whether such a Saint Nicholas would scare her now. "And he'll come tomorrow?" she asked timidly.

"That man? How could he? He's still back there, over the ocean. And nobody from Sedalia would probably come this far out, either. So you are safe."

Tilli wasn't quite sure she was glad or sorry. She thought she had been a good girl this year. Why, when she left them, even the usually cross Baelks had said she was a good child! And Mother never whipped her as they'd done. It would be nice to have some sweets, especially after all the plain meals every day.

But she sighed and tried to forget about tomorrow.

The next morning she was aroused by Mother's calling. "Wake up, birthday girl! Do you want to sleep this late forever? You know, what you do on your birthday, you're likely to do all year."

Tilli didn't know about that. She immediately told Lotti that they both must be very careful today.

"Besides," Mother was saying, "you just might want to see what Saint Nicholas left for you."

So he had come, after all! Well, it didn't take Tilli long to slip on her clothes and clatter down the ladder.

"What did Saint Nicholas bring?" she asked before she'd left the last rung.

"Not so impatient, there!" Mother scolded, but pleasantly. "First, your birthday spanking."

"Oh," Tilli told herself, "now it will come! Saint Nicholas must have left a switch!"

"Turn around," Mother ordered. But there seemed to be a chuckle in her voice.

Tilli hunched over for the first strike.

"One!" Mother counted in English, as she tapped Tilli lightly where spankings usually go. "Two! Three!" She accompanied each number with a tap, all the way up through "eight!" And then there was a slightly harder tap as Mother sang out, "And one to grow on!" Then she gave Tilli a quick, tight squeeze: "Happy birthday, *Mädchen!*"

"Me, too! Me, too!" Melia had come down and was jumping about excitedly. "I want to be counted!"

35

"Oh, your birthday's a way off," said Mother, "a long, long way yet."

Would that be the same as the "long, long time" before they'd be going to school? Tilli wondered.

Melia's happy look had faded.

"But maybe," Mother was saying, "your sister will share what Saint Nicholas brought her." Here Mother went to the cupboard and lifted out a plate piled with brown gingerbread men, complete with arms and legs and raisin eyes.

Tilli gasped. They looked just like the cookies (oh, so good!) that Mother gave them when they had first arrived from the Old Country. But Saint Nicholas must indeed have brought these, Tilli reasoned. For how could Mother make cookies when there was so little sweet molasses left? Mother had told her it took molasses to make cookies.

Father, too, gave Tilli a gentle "spanking" when he came in. Then he swung her up toward the ceiling until she shrieked in half fear, half delight.

"It won't be too much longer that I can do that with our girl," Father said, breathing hard. "She's getting so big!"

The cookies topped off breakfast for everyone. Tilli hardly knew which part of her second gingerbread man to start eating. She finally decided to save the whole face till noon.

And all day she went about as in a magical world. She was growing up to be a big girl. If only she didn't get too big for school!

That evening before she said good-night to Lotti and dozed off, she heard Father and Mother singing together again. That made her feel warm through and through.

The song was one of Tilli's favorites, *"Liebesprobe."* It began with sweethearts saying good-bye under a tall linden tree. The young man had to start his long years of wandering as a journeyman, and the two pledged true love for the hard separation. Over the lonely years the girl yearned for his return.

But when that happened and he came riding a fine horse, she didn't recognize him. And he wanted to find out whether she was still gentle-hearted and loving. That's why he pretended he had just been in a neighboring village at the wedding of her sweetheart. He asked her what wishes she wanted to send for the man's future.

Tilli wondered what she would do if she had been the unhappy girl. Of course, she knew the outcome. But each time she heard the question sung, she held her breath in suspense till the answer came. It took stanza after stanza. Tilli thought each more beautiful than the last:

> *"I send him as many good wishes as droplets fall in the rain,*
> *As droplets fall in the rain!"* . . .

> *"I wish him as much good fortune as heaven is sprinkled with*
> *stars,*
> *As heaven is sprinkled with stars!"* . . .

> *"I pray him as many honors as sand grains cradle the sea,*
> *As sand grains cradle the sea!"*

Tilli's chest swelled as she thought how very good that girl was. Then came the most exciting question:

> *"What is it he takes from his finger?"*

And next the thrilling answer:

> *"A ring of the finest red gold!"*

Tilli always swallowed hard at this point, even though the man then revealed who he was, begged his true love to dry her tears, and gave her the ring, already inscribed with their names.

How glad Tilli was that he had found that girl truly faithful and good. And what a narrow escape it was for the girl! For her sweetheart told her at the very end:

> *"Had you sent hateful words, or sworn,*
> *I'd have ridden away and never returned."*

But everything had turned out right. Tilli breathed deeply and smiled as she held Lotti close.

It was her very first remembered birthday, and such a truly happy one!

Chapter 5

The molasses, however, was soon really gone. The cornmeal from the few ears the family could find was getting low in the big tin bucket by the cupboard. The catfish seemed to know where to hide under the ice; the rabbits, how to escape to their burrows. Parts of the potatoes—"eyes," Mother called them—had to be saved for starting a new crop in the spring. The nuts didn't go into *Kuchen* but were rationed out to each person in small portions. Without money, there soon wouldn't be even beans, and surely books would be out of the question.

Tilli's worries grew over whether the family would soon be without food and they'd all be hungry as she had often been. She heard what happened when Father tried to buy something on credit from a store in town. He was still boiling.

"To me—Anton—" he shouted, pointing fiercely at his chest, "that man says, 'Nobody takes anything out of this store without paying cash for it.' "

Father scowled, imitating the storekeeper. "As if I were a common thief! He talks that way to me! The others get credit. But I! To him I'm just a poor, dumb Dutchman!" he ended furiously.

Mother extended both palms in his direction. "Shhhhh, Anton! Think of the children."

"I am thinking of the children!" Father stormed. "Well, I'll show him! We've never starved yet, and, by thunder and lightning, we never will! I can work—hard. We worked hard enough in that greenhouse in Brooklyn when we first landed from the Old Country. And there's still that brickyard in Sedalia where I worked to get money for this farm." He was getting louder and louder. "What's more, I was a much bigger greenhorn then than I am now. I'll show that smart-aleck storekeeper! And I'll never buy another thing from him as long as I live!"

Mother looked distressed. "Never is a long time." She sighed.

But Tilli felt like clapping. She was very proud of Father.

Before too many days Tilli found that he meant what he said about working in town. He was no longer home much, except at the end of each week. And then sometimes Mother, too, went with him. She'd work some days doing housework for families in Sedalia.

Albert was left to take care of the stock. Because the cow was dry, there was no need for Tilli to struggle with milking. She and Melia played with their dolls in the cabin or on warm days out on the big rock, until even that got tiring. After all the usual lively talk at table and the happy singing when Mother and Father were home, Tilli now felt strangely empty. It was almost like the lonely times in the Old Country when she had been alone with the Baelk children.

When Mother came home, she was usually tired but had a glint in her eyes. "The ladies pay well," she'd say, pulling some coins out of her skirt pocket. "And see here,"—she'd smile as she held up a pair of brass-toed shoes or a shaggy coat and trousers—"the lady gave me these."

The hand-me-downs went up on a growing pile in the loft.

"I think I can cut this," Mother said one day, measuring up on Tilli a drab gray skirt, "to fit you for when you go to school."

School! How Tilli's heart bounced! Mother had used the magic, but almost forbidden word!

"I'm going to school!" Tilli began to shout, to nobody in particular. "When? When, Mother?"

"Not so jumpy, my little frog," Mother scolded, still holding up the skirt. "All in good time."

How could Tilli keep still when all her wonderings about going to school were suddenly popping inside her?

"When?" she asked again.

"I said, all in good time" was all Mother would tell her. But that didn't stop Tilli's mind from churning.

Back in Europe, she had wanted desperately to be allowed to attend the village school, even though there'd been terrible hints about what happened to children there. Yet she had always wondered: if the stories were really true, why would the Baelks plan to send their Mitzi?

In America surely school would be different. And how really wonderful it would be to learn so many things at last!

Of course, Tilli and Melia had already been learning about counting from Mother. Albert, too, had helped. With beans he laid out the shapes of numbers and letters as the girls learned to say the names. At those times Tilli was so busy she didn't notice whether he seemed cocky or not.

Each day Mother had occasion to explain the differences

between many English and German ways of saying things. She had been in America, oh, a very long time, Tilli imagined, working in that place called Brooklyn, and had found out many things herself. Only she couldn't read things in English. And not even Albert had any books. School would do all the teaching so much better, even magically, Tilli was sure.

Now, looking at the floppy skirt, she pushed aside all the other, bigger questions that were jostling in her mind.

"Wouldn't it need a top?" she asked.

Mother huffed. "Of course a top! And to cover that up, a hug-me-tight. What do you think I have been knitting these nights, a giant's stocking?"

Yes, Tilli knew Mother had been knitting. She knitted most evenings when she was home and wasn't carding wool or spinning it into hanks of yarn. Often it was after Tilli and the others were in bed. But other times there was a chance to watch. Tilli never tired of seeing the spinning wheel go round, or watching Mother guide the loose wool so that it twisted into strands of tight yarn to be looped into hanks for knitting. And she liked to help wind those into fat, squeezy balls.

"How could you ever learn to do all that?" she once asked when Mother was making the spinning wheel go so fast the spokes were lost in a blur.

"Easy enough," Mother answered, her foot continuing to move the treadle, "when you have a good teacher."

"In school?"

"Oh, no. Your grandmother was an expert. I learned from her."

Tilli would have begged right then and there to learn, too. But mention of a grandmother set her questioning in

42

another direction. "I had a grandmother?" she asked, astonished.

"Of course. How otherwise should I have had a mother?"

Mother stopped her work and was quiet a moment. At last she said, "You were of course too little to remember. But you were a favorite of hers, my girl. She used to ride you on her foot and sing songs to you."

Tilli wished she could remember those times. She squeezed her eyes tight, trying to make a memory come. But none did.

"I didn't even know I had a grandmother," she said. "Did I have a grandfather, too?"

Mother seemed to bristle. "Of course I had a father! A fine father—when he was sober. A count's son he was, I want you to know!"

"A count's son?" Tilli was nearly breathless. "Then—then you *are* a princess, after all!"

"Me, a princess?" Mother laughed strangely. "Hardly! To be a princess, you have to have a king for a father and a queen for a mother, or something like that." Mother's smile was crooked. "*My* mother was a commoner, and my father was disinherited."

The words baffled Tilli. "What does that mean— 'commoner' and 'dis——' what you said?"

"They mean things a little girl shouldn't worry her head over," Mother answered. "Besides, both your grandmother and your grandfather are gone now."

Mother picked up the wool again. "But, as I said, my mother was a fine spinner and knitter. When I was your age, it seemed to me she was spinning most of the time. And later—why, she was even spinning when your grandfather died!" Mother ended with a sigh.

"Oh—how?" was all Tilli could think to say.

"Well, he was in bed, very, very sick. But he could hear your grandmother singing a hymn—you know, to the rhythm of her spinning, the way I sometimes do."

Tilli knew. She loved to hear Mother sing as she spun the wool. "But what happened?"

"Well, first thing she knew, he was in the room, shouting at her, 'You think the devil is about to get me, do you?'"

Mother stopped to explain. "He must have been out of his head with the sickness, you understand."

Tilli didn't really, but she was eager to know the rest. "Then what?"

"Well, he just grabbed that spinning wheel and smashed it to splinters, right then and there. And that was it. He stumbled back toward his bed, but dropped dead before he reached it."

"Oh!" Tilli gasped. How terrible that would be! "What did you do?"

"Oh, I wasn't there. That was long after I'd left home to marry your father."

Tilli tried to imagine a time when Mother and Father hadn't been together. It was hard to do.

Suddenly Mother spoke very briskly. "Now you'd better forget everything I said about your grandfather. I've talked altogether too much. He was a good man most of the time. And he *was* a count's son—remember that."

Mother returned to her spinning. But she sat up very straight and held her head high.

Tilli thought that all she needed to be a princess was a shiny crown.

And no princess would go back on her word. If Mother

said Tilli was to go to school, it would come true . . . some day, all in good time.

She needed that belief to cling to, for nothing more was said about school in the days that followed. Mother finished the gray hug-me-tight, and the skirt, but still said nothing. Then she knitted a bright red cap for Tilli and a white hood for Melia. Still, school seemed no nearer.

As the slow, empty days dragged on, Tilli worried more and more. And the more she thought about what Father once had said about trying to walk, and about meeting herself coming back, the more she wondered. Maybe it wasn't really so far to Sedalia as it seemed that time. When Mother and Father went, they of course rode in the cart. But perhaps that was just because they usually seemed tired.

Every day the idea of trying to walk grew more inviting. It was like an itch that wouldn't go away. What an adventure it would be to see whether she could walk the distance, after all! And happiest of all was the thought that if she found it possible, then there surely wouldn't be any reason at all why she couldn't begin school right away!

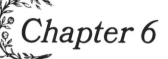

Chapter 6

Then a day came that really teased her to try. The late-winter sun was warm, and the very air seemed to say, "You can do it!"

Mother and Father were both gone. Maybe Tilli could even find them somewhere in Sedalia and come back with them. It couldn't hurt to try.

A nagging feeling told her not to go. But still, hadn't Father that time merely said she probably couldn't, not shouldn't, walk so far? That had been a while ago. Now she was so much older—over eight. And anyway, hadn't Father been only joking?

Albert was out somewhere experimenting with a rabbit trap he'd made. Melia had fallen asleep with her raggedy doll.

But just as Tilli was tiptoeing into the cabin for her new red cap, she heard Melia asking, "Where are you going, Tilli?"

Tilli meant to sound as though it weren't important. But she couldn't tell a lie, either. "Up the road," she said.

"Me, too!" Melia begged. "I want to go, too."

"You'll get tired."

"No, I won't. Please? I'll walk fast."

Tilli hesitated. This wasn't what she'd planned. But

Melia looked so eager, and they had shared so many other things together. "Well," Tilli said, "get your shawl, then, and your new hood."

Melia didn't bother with the hood, though. "It's sunny outside—see?"

It was warm for winter and a thoroughly lovely day. Only little patches of snow snuggled against the shady sides of the trees along the winding road.

Prickles of excitement stirred Tilli. She skipped happily on the places that weren't rutted, or picked her way carefully among the rocks at the side. Melia ran ahead when the way was downhill, but lagged behind when the way slanted steeply upward.

Soon she was panting and calling, "Wait, Tilli! Stop! I can't go so fast!"

Tilli wished she didn't have to be slowed up. To her the walking didn't seem hard at all. "Why don't you go back if you're already tired?" she urged her sister.

But Melia persisted.

Soon they were passing through heavy woods. A few dried leaves still hung on the oaks. The air was chill in the half-shade.

"I'm cold," Melia complained. "My ears—"

"Here, take my cap," said Tilli, tossing it over.

They followed the road as it continued to twist in and out and round about. Suddenly it plunged down into full sunlight again. It was sparkling back from the waters of a wide creek. Was it their very own creek? It seemed too far away for that. Tilli first squealed in delight. Then it was in disappointment. She had completely forgotten about this place. Those other times the wagon and the cart had crossed the water easily. But Tilli could see that she and Melia could never wade through so much water, even if they took off their shoes and tried.

To give up after such a good start! Why, they must be nearly to Sedalia by now! She stamped her foot in disappointment.

But Melia was laughing and skipping down to the water's edge. In the bright sunshine she had taken off Tilli's cap and was swinging it back and forth by its strap.

Tilli saw her suddenly stumble, just as the cap swung forward.

Melia righted herself at once. But the cap—the pretty, warm new one that Mother had spent so many nights knitting—landed in the water!

Tilli watched for a stunned, breathless moment. The flow of water started the cap moving slowly along the edge of the creek. Then it was caught against a dried cattail.

In seconds, Tilli's shocked numbness passed. She stomped quickly through the dead grasses to the edge of the water. She stretched toward the cap. But her arm was too short to reach it. She would have to step out on what seemed a snow-covered ledge. Just that much farther, she told herself, and the cap would be in her hand!

No sooner had she put her weight forward, though, than the whole bank crumpled under her. Her feet went down to over her shoe tops in the icy water. A chill shot through her. But she could almost touch the cap!

Just as she lurched forward to seize it, a swirl of water freed it from the closest reed and carried it to another a few inches away.

Tilli sloshed a few steps on, hands outstretched. Then she felt her feet slide. The cap floated free, and Tilli was jounced into still deeper water. She barely kept her balance. She screamed. She tried to stagger up the bank. There was nothing to hold on to. She slipped farther into the freezing water.

Melia was picking her way down to the creek's edge. "I'll help you, Tilli," she cried excitedly. "I'm coming to help you."

"No! No!" Tilli shouted with as much breath as she could spare. "Stay back! Stay back!"

Then Melia set up a loud wailing. "You're getting deeper!" she cried.

"Help! Help!" Tilli screamed in spite of herself. Who was there to help?

Once more she tried to get out of the hole she was in, but failed. The creek bottom was slippery. To keep her balance she spread her arms outward and forward. Now her hands and the fringes of her shawl were wet and cold.

Another attempt toward solid ground sent her lower than before. The bottom of her skirt was heavy with water. "Help!" she shrieked.

"Oh, Tilli, come back! Come back!" Melia was sobbing.

Then another, sharper voice broke in. "Melia! Tilli! Whatever are you doing here?"

Albert! There he was, stomping toward Tilli along the bank, the dripping red cap in his hand.

Tilli was too relieved at seeing him to wonder then how he happened to be there.

"Oh, help me, Albert! I keep slipping!" she begged, already beginning to shake with the cold.

Albert reached out one hand, then suddenly drew it back.

"First promise me—" he began.

Tilli was shivering and reaching out her hand. "Yes, yes," she gasped, "anything!"

"Promise you won't play any more tricks on me?"

"Oh, yes, I promise!" Tilli stammered.

"No fake squirrels, or anything like that?—Ever?"

"No—I mean yes, ever and ever!"

"Then hang on tight," Albert directed. He reached out his hand and braced his feet on a rock.

Tilli took his hand with both of hers. In a quick struggle, she staggered up on the firm bank.

"Look at you, silly!" Albert scolded. But he was shaking himself. Was he angry—or frightened, too? "What'll Mother say? You're all wet. Why, how foolish! You could have drowned!"

Tilli's teeth were knocking together. "Y-yes, I kn-know," she admitted, trying to shake the water from her skirt.

"You better get home as fast as possible," Albert continued. He sounded as severe as Father did sometimes.

Shivery as she was, Tilli had to know how far she had come. "Are we almost to Sedalia?" she managed to ask.

"Sedalia?" Albert whooped. "You must be crazy! Sedalia's miles and miles from here. Come on. You've got to get home."

Suddenly Tilli began to shake so, she couldn't see how her legs would ever take her there.

"It's too far!" she wailed.

"It's not far at all, this way. Come on!" Albert grabbed one of Tilli's icy hands and one of Melia's and led them. They stumbled along the creek bank. Tilli's feet were so numb she could hardly feel them moving. But she could hear her toes squishing inside her shoes. "It's all for nothing," she muttered, as she was half-pulled through the dead weeds and grasses. "I can't go that far."

"It's not far, I tell you," Albert insisted.

Sure enough! Before she knew, there was the hill with the nut and oak trees, then came the big rock, and, beyond, the little log house that was home. Tilli could hardly believe it.

"But we walked and walked such a long, long way, on the road!" Melia said it for them both.

"Oh, the road!" Albert said loftily. "That winds around like a snake. This is a shortcut I know."

Before she'd even started to dry off, Tilli asked the question that had been worrying her ever since she'd got safely out of the creek. "Will you tell Mother, Albert?"

"Of course, we have to tell Mother—and Father," he snapped.

Tilli was afraid to think about that. Now surely they would whip her. Worse yet, they probably would never love her anymore. She would lose the dearest part of being in America.

She was so cold inside and out, it seemed nothing could make her warm. Melia helped her out of the soggy shoes and brought their featherbed down to her.

Albert kept asking, "What in the world got into you to go off like that?"

Miserable though she was, Tilli did not answer. She would not tell and have him laugh at her or scold her again!

When she finally heard the cart clatter into the shed lot, she began to shiver uncontrollably. Albert rushed out. Now he'd tell them, she knew.

Father was the first to break into the room. His eyes were

fiery as he stared at Tilli where she cowered in the featherbed. "Thunder and lightning, child!" he shouted. "What were you doing over there?"

Tilli could only whimper. She expected a whipping then and there.

"Tell me!" Father demanded. Was he angry or afraid? "I want the truth, Tilli."

That meant only one thing to her: He trusted her; she had to tell him. "I wanted to see if I couldn't walk . . . to school. . . . And not meet myself coming back, the way you said," she ended lamely. She held her shoulders to try to still their quivering. She hunched down, waiting for the blows to come, as had so often been the way with the Baelks.

Instead of striking out, Father paced the floor a moment. Then he rushed to her and gave her a quick, hard hug. "My girl, my girl!" he muttered. "God in heaven, you could have been drowned, *Liebchen!*"

Tilli didn't have breath to agree.

Next thing she knew, she heard the door bang open.

"Albert told me," Mother said grimly and slammed the door shut.

Tilli hesitated to look up at her. But she had to see. Mother's mouth was set in a firm, straight line. In another second she was kneeling beside Tilli, feeling her forehead, then her hands, and finally her numb feet.

Then she stood up. "What are you standing around helpless for, Anton? The girl's about frozen. We have to get a fire going—and hot water. Quick, Albert! Out with you for some corncobs! And soak them in coal oil so they'll burn faster! Melia, up to the loft for that bunch of dried blossoms! We have to make some tea."

Still no whipping, thought Tilli, as she tried to prevent her teeth from chattering.

Mother bustled about, hurrying Father with the fire-making. Tilli only half heard her intense questioning and his answers between curt directions, then the sounds of lids being lifted and closed and kettles clattering on the stove.

In between, Mother came over again to rub Tilli's hands and feet. "*Ach,* that it should mean so much to you!" she blurted out, shaking her head.

Tilli was puzzled. But Mother seemed too busy to say anything more.

Finally Tilli's feet were tingling in a basin of hot water. Chills still surged through her, in spite of the careful way Mother had tucked the featherbed around her.

Then Mother brought over a mug of steaming *"Flieder"* tea. It was made from elderberry flowers and smelled pleasant. Carefully Mother drew a chair close and eased herself into it. She put an arm around Tilli and held the tea in the other hand so that Tilli could drink.

"Sip it as fast as you can, child," Mother ordered.

Tilli tried. It was very hot, but it tasted sweet and good. With each sip she could feel the warmth spreading inside her.

When the mug was empty, Tilli discovered the tightness was almost gone. It was such a relief to be warm and safe! But instead of being glad, she was suddenly sobbing; she couldn't tell why.

Mother was still holding her. But what was she thinking, and what would she do next?

"I only wanted to save my new red cap," Tilli said, shaking with each sob, "the one you worked so hard to make."

Mother herself seemed to catch back a sob. *"Mädchen, Mädchen!"* she said, holding Tilli still closer. "It was only a cap!"

Mother's voice was muffled and a bit hoarse. But Tilli thought it must be the way angel talk sounded. Mother still loved her!

Chapter 7

When it was about over, it seemed that the winter had not been so bad as Father had first feared. There was no milk, but Mother sometimes brought special foods from the people where she worked. The nut crock emptied out, but there might be sweet prunes to chew after the monotonous meals of beans or potatoes.

The warm days came oftener. The snow completely melted into the ground or off the dead leaves in the woods. And Father brought home mushrooms he'd found or silver fish from the creek.

Tilli and Melia watched every day for new things sprouting from the soil or the branches of the trees. Redbuds spread their pink umbrellas overhead, and white dogwood seemed to float like filmy scarves among the tree trunks. Little pink blooms, spring beauties, grew at the base of the oaks, and purple swaths of violets lay on the open hillsides. Each kind of tree, as it began to leaf out, showed a different color, Tilli noticed—yellow, green, red, orange, even pink. All outdoors was beautiful.

"Look!" Melia would say, linking two violet heads together and pulling till one broke off.

And "Look!" Tilli would exclaim as she stuffed dandelion

stems together to make a chain. "See, a crown!" She joined ends to make a yellow circle for Lotti's or Melia's head.

One morning it was Father's turn to call to the girls. "Come! I want you to see something." He motioned them from their favorite play place, the big rock by the pool, to follow him to the shed.

While still outside they could hear Bossy mooing softly. And when they peeked into the shed, there, curved beneath Bossy's head, was a woolly little calf. Bossy's tongue was busy licking the baby's coat this way and that. The red and white hair was standing straight out in some places and lying down, wet and flat, in others. The calf kept nuzzling against its mother.

"Why does it do that?" Melia asked.

"Oh," said Father, "it's already hungry and wants some milk."

"How will it get any milk?" Melia wondered aloud.

Tilli knew, but she let Father tell. He laughed. "How did we get milk from Bossy before? But this little fellow will have to wait a bit. Your mother has stripped out all of the first milk. And soon—maybe by tomorrow—the milk will be right for her to make big pancakes for us."

He smacked his lips so that his mustache waved, and he lifted his eyebrows extravagantly. "I've already bought her the flour."

He was right. The very next morning Mother was smiling as she worked over the stove.

"Now you will see some good eating!" Father said, rubbing his hands together as if he were going to produce some magic.

Tilli watched, fascinated, as Mother put some fat into the

big iron skillet and spread it around with the back of a spoon. Then she quickly dipped several spoonfuls of batter into the skillet, tilted it, and kept turning it in a circle. The batter flowed toward the edges and filled the whole bottom of the skillet.

Mother set the pan back on the stove, and after a few moments flipped over a big browned cake. Almost as soon, she was lifting it out. "Who wants the first one?" she asked teasingly.

"Me!" said Tilli.

"Me!" "Me!" came from Melia and Albert.

"It goes to your father," Mother announced firmly as she plopped the pancake onto the plate he held out to her. "Who bought the white flour? And who helped Bossy have her calf?" Already Mother was starting another pancake.

The process went on as before. Tilli was so excited watching that she almost missed her turn. But when she had her first bite of the crusty edges and the rich, tender inside, she thought this must be what princesses have to eat every day.

And the big pancakes weren't the only wonderful things Mother made, now that there was milk again, and a few eggs from the hens Father got in trade for wood he'd chopped. Tilli especially liked the sweet prune soup and the chunky noodles—*Klitze,* Mother called them.

Sometimes the noodles were fried in butter made from Bossy's cream—mmmmm! At other times Mother turned them into another kind of sweet soup.

Tilli thought it was magical the way Mother managed to make them. Her hands worked so fast, as she used a knife to slice off, from her tilted bowl, bits of soft dough into the boiling water. The bits puffed up into tiny dumplings of all shapes and tasted wonderfully good after the rich milk and the sugar were added.

Yes, Tilli thought happily, Father had promised no one would starve, and he was ever so right! Surely Mother's promise about school would come true, too.

She was home more now, helping Father and Albert get the fields ready for planting.

"Come, Tilli—and Melia, too. You're not too little to hand me the potato eyes," Mother called one morning.

So it was that everyone helped plant the potato parts saved from the winter supply. Father thrust the spade down into plowed ground and shoved it to one side so that Mother or Albert could push the potato piece deep down and hold it there till Father pulled his spade out again to let the ground slip over the planting. Tilli and Melia thought it fun always to be ready with a piece for each hole Father opened up. Then he would stamp the ground firm and move to the next space.

Later there was corn to put out in the biggest field. And Tilli was allowed to plant some of the beans, too, in the middle of very straight rows. She was careful to plant them with their "eye" sides down and separated by a space the width of her hand. Sometimes she was slow because she practiced her counting as far as she had learned, as she put down each bean.

"It will be a better winter next time," Father promised after all the planting was done.

But Tilli soon discovered there was yet a lot of work to do before that promise would come true. Weeds had to be pulled, beans hoed, lumps cracked, corn hilled up, and growing weeds chopped off.

Father was often working in town again, and Mother, too. That meant Tilli had to help Albert with much of this work.

It would be so much, much nicer to be going to school! Could Mother have forgotten? Surely not Mother! Yet it seemed like forever that Tilli had been waiting. Maybe Tilli ought to remind her, but not so that Mother would think Tilli didn't believe her.

"In Sedalia," she asked one day, "do you always see the children at school?"

"In school, now?" Mother asked in surprise. "No, *Mädchen,* there is no school now. The children are home in the summertime, helping with the work, no doubt."

My, Tilli was relieved! She hunched her shoulders up and grinned to herself. So she wasn't missing anything now! Suddenly her chores were more like fun.

The little calf, so wobbly on its legs at first, soon became a sturdy walker. Tilli helped him learn how to drink skimmed milk from a pail instead of getting his meals directly from his mother. In that way the family could have more milk to drink and more cream for butter.

As Mother directed her, Tilli first got the calf to suck on a finger or two. He must be a little silly, Tilli thought, to confuse fingers with teats! But she liked the tickle as the calf's mouth closed over her fingers and he began to suck noisily. Then she would slowly move her hand down into the pail of milk. As he kept working at the fingers, he couldn't help taking swallows of milk.

Sometimes he got too big a gulp at once and started to choke as he pulled his head out of the pail. Tilli giggled. He looked so funny with his whiskery nose all frosted white and wet! Then she would begin all over again.

After a few times he learned to suck easily on Tilli's fingers. And before too long he didn't even need such a starter, but could swallow the milk directly. When the pail was nearly empty, Tilli had to be very careful to hold it firmly, or in his eagerness for the last swallows, he might butt both the pail and Tilli over on the ground!

Soon he was having meal mixed in with the milk. And within several weeks he was also nibbling at the grass and the dandelions out in the pasture with his mother. He was getting big, and as round as Mother's new butter churn.

As the summer days grew shorter, there was harvesting to be done. The beans had dried in their pods. They had to be picked from the crackly bushes, then shelled and sorted. Under the coal-oil lamp on the table, Tilli spread a handful of beans at a time and looked them over carefully, pushing aside any that were brown or had holes. The good ones went into flour sacks for Mother to tie up. The others could be used to practice shaping letters or numbers. It was good to know most of the English names by now.

When Father and Mother were home, they dug out rows of potatoes. Melia helped Tilli pick up the fat tubers and dump them into bushel baskets.

Long since, the corn had grown tall, with tassels topping each stalk. Now the drying leaves rustled in the wind. Almost every stalk carried one or two heavy ears ready for husking.

"This time," Father announced one morning, "we will not bother to make shocks. We will husk the ears right from the standing corn and put them into sacks ready to take with us."

Tilli's ears pricked up. What did Father mean—"take with us"? "Where?" she asked.

"Why," Father said, a twinkle in each eye, "to town as soon as we get the harvesting and butchering done. We can't let you children put off school any longer."

My, Tillie felt sparkly inside! Now Father, too, had promised school! The magic must be coming true. Only—

"Where will we live?" she asked. "Where can we go?"

"In a house, of course, my little flutterbug! Do you think we would live in a cave like so many elves?"

Tilli couldn't answer. She was almost exploding with excitement. Then she suddenly thought of Mother. She must tell Mother this wonderful news!

Panting from her run, she found Mother in the loft sorting clothes.

"Mother!" she cried, "we are going to another house!— in the town!" Then, when there was no answer and Mother turned around, Tilli announced more firmly, "Father said so, just now."

"Really?" Mother dragged out the word. She seemed very much surprised. "Are you sure?"

"Yes, he said so, really. I wanted to tell you so you'd know, too. And we're going to school!"

Then Tilli saw that Mother was holding back a big smile. "You knew already!" The fun of telling began to desert Tilli.

"Why, of course I knew, child! Your father and I both decided you must go to school. Now, did he tell you anything about the house?"

"No, just that it wasn't a cave."

Mother laughed. "Well, it's a nice brick house, right on Grand Avenue. The bricks were part of your father's pay. Another man helped with the building. You will see how much better it is than this log hut, my little nosy-posy."

Tilli felt suddenly hollow, trying to imagine leaving. "What will happen to everything here?"

"It won't run away. Your father's having a man farm this place while we are gone. In that way we'll have part of the crops for food, you children will go to school, and we'll all live in a nice house together."

Tilli tried to picture it all, but it was almost too much to imagine at once. Everything wonderful seemed to be falling in place for her and her family. Mostly, now it was so near, she wondered what going to school would be like.

Mother was holding her head proudly. "Your father is very clever—don't you forget that. And in town we can both work more. Many people there want help."

Mother seemed to be talking more to herself than to Tilli. "Maybe," she finished, "we will even earn enough to buy more land."

Chapter 8

How exciting it was to be in the new house and to have the happy prospect of school, too!

As Mother said, the house was on Grand Avenue, and Tilli thought it, too, was grand. It had red bricks outside and smooth walls inside. The floor was of boards, rough but level. And it had three rooms besides the big one where the stove for cooking was. One room held the sacks of corn and beans from the farm. In another were the husk mattresses for the children. Mother and Father had a room to themselves. At first Tilli went around counting, "One—two—three—four!"—in English, of course.

The very first day, though, she still had that strange, empty feeling whenever she thought of the familiar loft with the low window looking out to where the golden fish were swimming and to the tree-covered hill where nuts were peppering down to the ground.

Here, from out the front window with its big panes of glass, there were new things to see. Tilli watched, all a-tingle, as children went skipping by as they came from school, dragging books held together by leather straps. There were also fine carriages with sleek horses stepping proudly along the street, and delivery wagons with writing on the sides.

Albert was quick to spell out and pronounce some of the words—"Lumber"—"Drugs"—"Furniture." How wonderful, Tilli imagined, it would be soon to be able to read all of them herself! She could hardly wait to start learning at school.

"When can we start?" she asked Mother, before they'd all had supper that first day.

"Well, Albert is to begin on Monday. But your dresses— I haven't had time to sew the buttons on them yet."

"Couldn't I do that?" Tilli wanted to know.

"And break a needle? Needles cost money, child. No, I'm afraid you'll just have to be patient a little while longer. Besides, your father has to talk to the teacher first."

"But Albert—? You said Albert—" Tilli began.

"Albert can do his own talking. He has been to school before."

Tilli knew that only too well. How often he had boasted about going in Europe.

So there was nothing Tilli could do but wait.

"Oh, that is a fine school!" Albert shouted when he came home the first day. "You should see all the books on the shelves! And see, here's the one I'm to use. Father gave me the money for it." He held it up proudly. "And I've got this slate—and the pencil for it. You can write things and then just wipe them off."

He started to demonstrate. It was marvelous to watch, but Tilli was even more interested in something else. "But, Albert, how was it? How did you get along?"

"Oh, some of the others laughed. They're such children! But the teacher thinks I speak English very well. I told him I had studied it in my German school. He looked mighty surprised, I can tell you!"

"Was it all very hard?" Tilli asked.

"Hard? Oh, well, the class is ahead, of course. They've been in school since September. But I'll catch up."

Tilli asked the next question in almost a fearful whisper. "Did anyone get whipped?"

"No—no whippings."

Tilli let out a long breath.

"But one stupid fellow had to stand in a corner of the room with a fool's cap on his head."

"Oh!" Tilli gasped. "Why?"

"He deserved it! He didn't really know anything."

"What's that crowing I hear?" said Father, coming into the room. "Just be sure you aren't the next to be made a fool of."

Albert shrugged. But Tilli shuddered. Surely she would be made to stand in a corner. She knew so little!

When the time finally came that Mother announced the girls would start the next morning, Tilli was almost quivering. Now that it was really going to happen, after such a long, long time of just wishing, she was almost more afraid than glad and excited.

What if she found school as terrible as some people in Europe had said it was? Or so hard that she couldn't possibly do well and would have to stand in the corner all day, or be sent home forever? Was it true, as Albert said, that no one got whipped? She wondered about Mitzi way across the ocean, and the children she saw passing the house. Were they afraid? What would tomorrow really be like? Tilli could barely get to sleep that night.

When Father led the girls past the schoolyard the next morning, Tilli kept sneaking glances at the many boys and girls racing and shouting happily at their games. Surely, she thought, there couldn't be many left inside standing in corners! She walked less fearfully.

And meeting their teacher made Tilli feel even better. Her welcoming smile reminded Tilli of the nurse at the dock after she left the ship. The teacher talked to Father, who in turn explained to the girls, "You'll be in with some beginners, she says, because of your late start. But if you work hard—"

He didn't need to finish. "Oh, I will, I will!" Tilli promised.

"Me, too," Melia echoed.

The teacher smiled quickly and led the girls to a desk that was big enough for two. "Just sit here," she motioned.

Father handed each of the girls a surprise—a slate and slate pencil just like Albert's, and to Tilli a new book!

"Now be good girls—and good students!" was Father's farewell as he left the room with the teacher.

Everything was so very strange that Tilli was more than a little scared. But she couldn't let Melia know.

"Here," she whispered, though no one else was there to hear, "try the slate and pencil, this way, see? It's like Albert's, only these are ours and we can use them. So he can't stop us. Try yours—like this—" Tilli made sample lines and rubbed them off with the side of her hand. Soon Melia was giggling as she tried the same thing and found that it worked.

Tilli took a hurried look at the wonderful things in the room about her. There were the other desks, all double like hers, a picture on the wall of a stern man with white hair, a flag at the front, a shelf with books just as Albert had said, and a big desk for things the teacher had put there when the girls arrived.

Then Tilli turned to examine her book, her very own schoolbook at last, to be shared only with Melia! She moved her fingers over its neat cloth cover, smelled the strong, clean scent of new print, tried to figure out the writing on the outside. She recognized the bigger letters! Then she peeked inside. Oh, there were colored pictures on some of the pages!

The first one she studied was of a little girl in a frilly blue dress. She was laughing as she rode high in a swing. There was writing below the picture. Here, too, she could name some of the letters, even though they were much smaller than the ones Albert had laid out with beans. How could Tilli wait until she learned what this writing said?

Next she found a picture of a dear baby bird standing on the edge of a nest. What was he about to do? Would the writing underneath tell? A mother or father bird was sitting on a nearby branch. And again there were lines of writing. Oh, how exciting it will be to learn what they say, Tilli thought happily. It would be hard, of course. But she wouldn't care about that at all, just so she could learn.

Suddenly a shrill bell rang somewhere, jarring her back to the present. Boys and girls began tumbling into the room. Tilli peeked up at them curiously. They looked much smaller than she was, or even Melia. Some glanced quickly her way. But most of them kept talking to one another, even as they settled at their desks.

Before long the teacher appeared at the door.

Immediately the hubbub stopped. And when the teacher went to her big desk, everybody scrambled out of his seat and stood up.

Tilli pulled Melia out to stand, too.

"Good morning, class!" said the teacher brightly.

"Good morning, Miss Gibson!" the children chorused back.

Tilli knew about "good morning," but to her the teacher's name sounded like "Give Some," and for a long time afterward she thought that was correct.

The children sat down. Miss "Give Some" pointed to words written in white on a big black wall. "Copy each of these ten times," she directed.

Tilli watched the other children taking out slates and slate pencils from the shelves under their desk tops, and begin writing. Soon all the sound she could hear was the scraping of slate on slate.

She took her pencil, too, and motioned Melia to do the same. But what should she do next? After a while Miss "Give Some" came to her and explained with words and gestures that she should copy down the writing from the blackboard.

It was all very confusing, putting down things she didn't understand! But Tilli worked hard trying to make her writing look like what was up there. Many times she rubbed hers off again. She was glad each time that she could start again. But her writing didn't look much neater than Melia's.

Miss "Give Some" frowned when she came by and examined what Tilli had copied. Tilli's heart thumped loudly. Would she have to stand in one of the corners now?

But Miss "Give Some" only took Tilli's pencil and changed a line or a curve here and there, each time saying, "See?—this way."

Tilli tried still harder with the rest of the words. Her fingers were pinched, and her tongue strained from moving at the same time as her slate pencil. Another bell rang, and the teacher announced, "Class dismissed."

With a rumble of slates shoved into desk shelves, the children stomped out of the room.

Tilli stayed in her seat until Miss "Give Some" came to explain and to point. "It's recess time, girls—playtime. Go on out with the others."

Tilli pulled Melia up from her seat and tugged her along behind a few stragglers to the playground. Tilli remembered vividly how she had envied the children playing here when she first passed the school so long ago. Now here she was, one of them!

Some boys and girls were already forming a circle and chanting a jolly song.

Two girls in swirly skirts skipped over to Tilli and Melia. "You're new, aren't you?" the girls chimed together.

Tilli thought she knew what they meant. She nodded.

One girl asked saucily, "Know how to play?" And she rattled off what sounded like "Rock the Sameron as round we go."

Tilli couldn't understand. She shook her head slowly.

The other then tried. "How about Andy Over? Ring Around a Rosy? London Bridge? Mulberry Bush?"

Tilli kept shaking her head. Nothing they were saying made any sense to her. She looked desperately for Albert. But he was on the far side of the playground, acting as if he didn't know her at all.

"Know any games at all?" one of the girls asked, her voice rising to a high pitch. The other girl snickered.

Tilli felt her eyes beginning to sting. She turned her face away.

One girl laughed shrilly and said to her friend, "They must be just some of those dumb Dutchmen." They both tittered, then turned to skip away.

Tilli understood the last only too well. "Let's get far away from those smarties!" She jerked Melia back to their classroom desks and they began copying again:

au-tumn leaves
sum-mer show-ers
spring beau-ties . . .

When the class returned, Miss "Give Some" gave out new directions. Tilli saw the other children take out books like her own. They all seemed to know what to do and began turning pages. Melia looked questioningly to Tilli. But Tilli couldn't help. Finally a girl across from her smiled, reached over, and flipped pages in Tilli's book till she stopped at one page and pointed. It was without pictures.

"Thank you, Sarah," Miss "Give Some" said, smiling at the girl who had helped Tilli find the right place. "I should have done that."

She then pointed to a boy whose desk was near the front of the room. He rose and began stuttering while he slowly moved his finger along the page of his book. Tilli thought what he was saying sounded something like "Twing-ul, twing-ul, leet-ul stair."

Tilli tried to guess where on her page he was reading from. She kept staring at the writing, but things didn't look like anything Albert had yet shown her. There was no way she knew to match the writing with what was being read.

70

As other children were called to read, Sarah again tried to point out the right place. But it was no use! Tilli was completely baffled, and a terrible heaviness pressed on her. How would she ever learn? Were all her wonderful hopes impossible?

Later that day Miss "Give Some" put numbers on the board. Almost at the very first, something began to tingle happily inside Tilli. Why, she could recognize those! The teacher then called several boys and girls in turn to come forward to "do sums," right in front of all the others.

At the start Tilli was frightened for each one, imagining what it would be like to be up there herself. But, once she realized what was happening and what the + sign meant, she didn't feel lost. It was just like those times at home when they'd all played games of counting and adding as they sorted beans or collected nuts. Tilli was almost itching to go up front herself.

This part of school was going to be exciting fun!

When Tilli and Melia were next out on the playground, Sarah was again helpful. She tried to explain about some of the games, even though Tilli couldn't understand. Sarah also pointed to some of the other girls and told their names. Soon several were gathered around Melia and Tilli, telling them the English words for things about the playground.

And slowly, as days went by, Tilli and her sister learned, by watching, how the games were played. Gradually, too, they were urged by Sarah's friends to join in with the rest of the children.

Even when the words didn't mean anything to them, it was fun to try copying the motions of the others. Tilli learned quickly that when the "bridge" fell down on the shoulders of someone skipping through the arch of arms, he was a captive and had to go to a "dungeon" for the rest of the game. She was often that "victim."

> *"Here's a prisoner we have got,*
> *We have got, we have got.*
> *Here's a prisoner we have got,*
> *   My fair lady!*
>
> *"Take the key and lock him up,*
> *Lock him up, lock him up . . ."*

Tilli didn't know who the fair lady was, but she guessed she must be a princess in a castle above a dungeon.

In another game, everyone stood in a big circle while one skipped in and out as everybody sang,

> *"Go in and out the window,*
> *Go in and out the window,*
> *Go in and out the window,*
> *As we have done before.*
>
> *"Now stand and greet your partner,*
> *Now stand and greet your partner . . ."*

Tilli thought most of the girls looked like princesses in their frilly skirts as they ducked under the upheld arms or went "in and out," laughing and singing.

But when her turn came, she wished she didn't have to take it. Her straight, gray made-over Mother Hubbard was no princess's gown. And her clumsy, hand-me-down brass-toed shoes clattered as she tried to skip lightly like the others. It was hard to be happy when something inside felt

as heavy as those boots! She wished her feet hadn't grown
so. Her first leather shoes were much too tight now. Melia
was wearing them.

Tilli practiced the songs, though, on the way home.
Sometimes imagining her coarse dress was pretty and lacy,
she tried the skipping dances by herself. She and Melia
helped each other remember words, even though they
usually didn't know what they meant.

> *"Intry, mintry, cutry corn,*
> *Apple seed and apple thorn,*
> *Wire, briar, limber lock,*
> *Three geese in a flock.*
> *One flew east, one flew west,*
> *And one flew over the cuckoo's nest!"*

They would count each other off to see who would be "It."
Then they'd laugh because there was no one else with whom
to play a game.

One rainy day, when recess had to be held indoors, the
boys and girls played Drop the Handkerchief in the hall.
When the bell rang, and everyone was settled in his seat,
Miss Gibson picked something up from the floor.

"Whose is this?" she asked, holding it up very cautiously
by only two fingers as if it might bite her.

It was a man's torn, stained, once-white handkerchief.
Tilli turned slowly to look at Melia. She recognized the
handkerchief as one of Father's that Mother had given to
Melia to use because there was nothing better.

Melia's face went red. Tilli felt her own getting hot.
What should she do—blurt out Melia's secret?

"Well?" Miss Gibson sounded impatient. She held the cloth still farther out from her.

Just when Tilli thought she couldn't hold a confession back one more second, Constance, one of the girls who always wore a fresh, pretty dress and a bow in her hair, raised her hand.

"Then come get it, please!" ordered Miss Gibson. And Constance did just that!

Tilli and Melia flashed startled, puzzled looks at each other. For many days afterward they wondered about Constance. She had seemed so rich! Why would she claim a grimy handkerchief that shamed Melia to silence? And sometimes they giggled together, knowing their little secret.

It made them feel less like "dumb Dutchmen," too.

Chapter 9

Gradually the copying began to mean something to Tilli. Often Miss Gibson stayed after school to help her pronounce groups of letters and whole words. It was a kind of puzzle-solving fun to discover words that matched those in her beautiful reader.

Many times she brought it home to sound out words letter by letter. Sometimes Albert helped her. Then again, he might laugh, just as they both did when they first heard Melia's strange, half-Polish talk so long ago.

"It's 'breāk,' not 'bree-ak,' you silly!" he might say. "Don't you know what a diphthong is?"

Of course Tilli didn't. And at times like that she was sure she would never learn to read correctly. But each time she tried again, until she got it right. What a wonderful feeling it was to be learning!

Since they were older than the rest of the class, Miss Gibson occasionally became impatient with her two "Dutchmen." But she never made them stand in the corner.

And somehow, before the violets were blooming in the neighboring woods and school was out, Tilli was able to read several little stories in her book. How often she chanted the rhymes about the girl in the swing and the little bird about to fly away! She knew those by heart. How proud and happy that made her!

Miss Gibson even let her take home with her over the summer a new speller and a different reader from the classroom shelf.

There wasn't as much time left over for study as Tilli would have liked, during those months. Even in town, there was a garden to tend, and sometimes the children were taken out to the farm to help the tenant there with the crops. And there was a new little brother, Feodor, to rock in his cradle. That gave Tilli a chance to sing all the new songs from school and the old, familiar ones she'd learned from Mother and Father.

What took most of her time was something quite different, however. Mother arranged for Tilli to help a town lady, Mrs. Hoffman, with housework and with watching her smallest child. It was a blue-eyed baby girl that reminded Tilli of the Baelks' Baby Gisela, the "Little Dumpling"—only this one lived in a very nice, big house.

What an exciting adventure it was for Tilli to skip along the streets toward the Hoffman house! Sometimes at Third Street she had to wait for the new streetcar to clatter by. It was pulled by mules and moved on iron tracks with a great deal of screeching. When the mules got stubborn, the driver let his whip go swinging above the long ears. Tilli always laughed then, remembering the balky horse that had delayed them all when she, Albert, and Melia first came home with Father.

At the start Tilli thought it was fine to work where everything was so "fancy." Dusting or doing dishes didn't seem like work at all there! Sometimes she was allowed to push the baby along the path in front of the Hoffman house.

How proud she was to be rolling such a splendid wicker baby carriage with its high wheels and umbrella top! And she loved to see the little pink face looking up from a still pinker, shiny satin pillow. It seemed to her that watching this baby girl, with her lovely, soft clothes, was even more fun than rocking Feodor, and nicer than holding Lotti. By now the doll was losing paint from her once rosy cheeks.

Inside, the Hoffman house was truly wonderful. When Tilli saw the lacy curtains, the deep-red portieres in the doorways, and the floors almost entirely covered with rose-patterned rugs, she was sure no castle could be more beautiful. The furniture was smooth and shiny. On the walls there were dark pictures in wide frames, and on one place in the parlor hung a puzzling machine.

Tilli was so curious, she had to ask Mrs. Hoffman what the queer oak box and the black hornlike things were.

"That's a telephone," she was told, "for talking to someone far away."

That seemed like magic. Tilli thought right off about Melia. She would like to tell her about this wonder now.

"How does it work? Could I—talk to my sister with it?"

"No, Tilli. I wish you could. I wish we all could. But it doesn't work at all now."

"Oh," said Tilli, letting that little word carry her big disappointment.

"It was really marvelous for a while," Mrs. Hoffman explained. "I could talk to anyone in Sedalia who also had a telephone."

"But . . . ?"

"But—you remember the sleet storm we had this spring?"

Tilli nodded vigorously. She and Melia had slipped and

skidded almost all the way to school that day when everything—trees, poles, bushes, roofs, grass, paths—was coated with clear ice.

"Well, that ice broke down most of the wires that made the telephones work. And they—at least this one—haven't yet been fixed. We hear rumors the company won't ever fix them."

So, for a talk with Melia, Tilli would have to wait. She didn't really see, anyway, how wires could let Melia hear anything from so many streets away.

There were occasional hours left from her work at the Hoffmans' for real talks with Melia, and good times, too. They tried lessons and often taught their dolls what they had learned at school, or made up stories of their own.

But Tilli could hardly wait for real school to begin again. Nice as their house was, what if Tilli had to go every day to the Hoffmans' forever?

How relieved she was to have Mrs. Hoffman say one morning, "Well, Tilli, I guess this will have to be your last day here. We can't have a little girl miss school. And that starts Monday."

Oh, what a whirl of excitement she was in on that first day of her second year! It was altogether different, going now, from that other time, when she didn't know what school or the other children would be like. Now she and Melia could shout, "Hello!" to friends and join immediately in the games before that first bell rang.

Other things were different during Tilli's second year. For one, she was no longer in the same room as Melia—only Melia wasn't called that now. Just about everybody at school was calling her Em or Emmy.

"What kind of a name is Melia?" some of her classmates

asked. "Besides, Em's easier." On the rare times that Albert noticed her on the school grounds, he echoed Father's even stranger use of her full name, Amelia.

But at home Mother huffed, "She's been Melia for years now. Changing is just plain foolishness!"

Tilli thought it best to side with Mother, at least at home. At school, it was whichever name seemed right at the time. Once, after Tilli mentioned Melia, a particularly haughty girl—one of those who at first had called the girls "dumb Dutchmen"—asked smartly, "You mean Emmy, don't you?"

Tilli was no longer cowed by such talk or fear of that girl.

"She's my sister," Tilli replied, her chin high, "and I use whatever name we like."

But her sister couldn't hear Tilli recite the "times-ies." Melia's class didn't even know about "times-ies" yet, even though Melia had learned some the year before. So Tilli had to find other girls, like Sarah, willing to hear her practice chanting in the school hallway:

> *"One times four is four.*
> *two times four is eight. . . .*
> *four times four is sixteen. . . ."*

or:

> *"Six times three is eighteen.*
> *seven times three is twenty-one. . . ."*

on and on.

Tilli could rattle off her "two times-ies" as easily as she now could sing all of "London Bridge." But when it was "five times" or even "four times," she stumbled or, worse yet, started naming some numbers in German instead of English! Then even her kindest classmates laughed.

"By next year," she kept promising herself, "I'll get them all right, for sure." If only she could be really sure!

Reading was going much better, and even spelling. Tilli would work till her fingers were cramped, trying to make her writing of words look the way her new teacher wanted. Oh, she was learning so many new and interesting things! It was like having a delicious supper after a long time of being hungry.

School! It made Tilli bubblingly happy just to know she was really there.

Everything at home, too, was, as Mother said, "heavenly."

Feodor was a busy, cheerful, healthy child, so different from poor Victor. Mother always looked proud and especially glad whenever she saw him. Tilli was tickly inside. It was so good to see her parents happy.

They worked hard each day, either at home or for someone else. But on special evenings they dressed up in clothes they never wore at any other time, and they went to a German club dance.

Mother's dress was the trim black one with the high collar and white bow Tilli knew from the picture on the front-room wall. It was the one Mother said had been taken in Brooklyn. To Tilli she looked beautiful dressed that way. And Mother's blue eyes would be crinkly with smiles as she got ready to leave.

Father, too, was especially jolly then, in his dark suit with the wide lapels. "We have to show these people," he said more than once, "that 'dumb Dutchmen' know how to have a good time. They just don't know how much more fun we all had in the Old Country than people here have!"

And the two would go off, half dancing already and singing, *"Ehe ich spazieren gehe."*

On some days, when Father wasn't working, he visited the court house and thought himself lucky if he could listen in on a trial. Tilli knew that when he came home afterward he'd always have something interesting to report.

He'd swing his arms about as he described the arguing that went on to determine who was in the right. "Such a liar that fellow was! I could tell in a minute," he'd say, pointing a finger and leaning over so far he almost touched Tilli's nose. "Not like my Tilli here, who always tells the truth."

Or he'd twirl his mustache with one hand and with the other clasp the lapel of his coat, to show how smug one lawyer had been. "Ha! It didn't do him any good to act so high and mighty. They sent his man to the calaboose!"

Father would smile broadly, then turn serious. "My, now! That would be something—to be able to do nothing but sit in a courtroom all day! But who would care to do all that studying first?" He sighed heavily.

Tilli didn't know about courts or lawyers. But she didn't think she could ever tire of studying. School was just the most wonderful place.

Then one Sunday Father came in with a startling, disturbing question: "Well," he began, "who wants to ride out with me to see our new farm?"

"Me!" squealed Melia. "Me, me!"

"I'll go," said Albert, "though of course I've already been there."

Father looked over to Tilli. "And what about my Tilli, my good little potato planter?"

A knot had started tightening inside her at the first mention of a new farm. Would they be going away from Sedalia—and school? She knew that some farms were right out on Grand Avenue, not very far from their brick house.

"Where—is it?" she asked. How dry her mouth was!

"Oh," Father boomed out proudly, "it's probably not so much as fifteen miles from where we stand right now."

Fifteen miles! Tilli thought that must be at least halfway back to Baltimore, where their ship had landed long ago. She could never walk to school from that far away!

She started to ask, "Then how will I—" But Father was continuing with what he thought his good news.

"Wait till you see it! It's on another branch of Flat Creek, just like the Morgan County place. Actually that's how I got such a good bargain. The creek's so close to the house—a real house it is, too!—that the man who owned the place was afraid it'd sweep the building away sometime. He must have no imagination at all, and I wasn't going to give him any of mine. He doesn't know I saw one house washed away in a flood—"

"I know!" Albert broke in. "I remember, the Vistula! And all the fishes flopping on the sand. They looked so funny!"

Father was not to be stopped. "—one house ruined," he continued, "and, by thunder and lightning, I'm not going to see another! I know a thing or two about taming a creek by now."

One half-happy wonder flitted through Tilli's mind. Maybe there would be golden fish there as at the other farm. But the alarm about school pushed that hope aside.

"Well," Father was beaming, "what say you?" His sparkly glance shot right at Tilli.

She had to look down at her toes. "What about school?" she mumbled.

"School?" Father echoed, as though it were the very first time he had ever heard the word. "Well . . . well . . . Oh, I guess there must be a school somewhere around there."

Tilli remembered there wasn't any school near the other farm. She turned to Mother for help. "But what if there isn't?" she half whispered.

Mother was staring down at her own hands. Her face seemed drawn and troubled. "Oh—" Mother made it sound unimportant. "We'll figure something out."

Then she looked up and said brightly, "Besides, you've already had more school than either I—or your father. You don't need to get smarter than we, now, do you?"

"Well . . . no. . . . No." Tilli could say that truthfully. She thought Mother and Father surely knew just about everything. But that didn't help her.

"That's my Tilli!" Father sang out.

Tilli's eyes were beginning to smart. "But—but—" That was all she could say.

Mother came over to pat her shoulder. "We're not moving till school is out, *Mädchen*. And by fall—who knows?"

Chapter 10

"She's the judge's wife, my girl!"

Mother was saying it as if it were a ginger-bread cookie dangled before Tilli's nose.

"But . . ." Tilli stopped. How could she ask again about going back to school, now that it *was* fall and the family was still at the new farm, so far from town?

Through the long summer weeks she had waited to learn what Mother and Father would do about letting her return to school. She had worked as hard as she could, she and Melia, gathering chips for the stove, helping plant potatoes and beans in the new fields, hoeing weeds out of the corn, doing some of the cooking, taking care of little Feodor so that Mother could help with the hay.

The only delightfully new part of the summer had begun with one of Father's surprises. It was early one morning that he brought into the kitchen a squirming pink creature.

"Here's something for you girls," he announced, holding it out in his cupped hands.

"What is it?" Melia asked.

Before actually seeing all of it, Tilli knew by its tiny squeals. It was a baby pig.

She rushed over to have a closer look. It was as hairless all over as Feodor's cheeks, and about as pink. Its eyes were closed, but it kept nuzzling Father's palm.

"Why is it doing that?" Melia wondered.

"It's hungry—that's why," Father explained. "He's the runt of the new farrow. He can't fight to get his share of milk from his mother."

Tilli hadn't even known that their sow was to have babies.

"What'll happen to him?" she asked. "Is he going to die, then?" She felt very sorry for the little pig if it was going to be that hungry.

"Not if you girls do your job right." Father laughed.

"Do what? How?" Melia asked, prancing about in her excitement.

Tilli was beginning to guess that she knew.

Father quickly explained how they should feed the little pig. Sure enough, it was much as Tilli had learned about teaching that first baby calf to drink milk. Only, of course, the piglet had a much smaller mouth and appetite and bowl.

"He has to have a name," Tilli announced when they were alone with their new charge.

"I know!" Melia suggested. "Let's call him Piggy."

"Oh, that doesn't sound nice!" Tilli protested. "When anyone gets called that at school, it means he's dirty or greedy. Didn't you ever hear that?" She was stroking the baby carefully. "And he's not that at all!" Tilli thought she had a perfect name in mind, but she was trying not to be pushy. "How about something to do with his corkscrew tail?"

"Oh, yes!" Melia said, clapping her hands. "Why not Curly?"

85

And that became his name, just as Tilli had hoped.

Curly quickly learned to drink milk and suck up mash. Soon he was romping around in the little pen the girls had made for him out of kindling sticks. When he got older, he was let to roam farther. But he always came running when he was called: "Curly! Curly! Curly!"

Tilli thought he was like a bouncing ball as he pricked up his pink ears, then came squealing and galumphing through the weeds and high grass. He would check from time to time to be sure he was aiming right, and finally arrive at his bowl, huffing from the effort and almost choking on his first eager swallows.

Before too long he was as roly-poly as his brothers and sisters and could join them at their trough or on acorn-hunting excursions. But Tilli and Melia still loved to call out, "Curly! Curly!" just for the fun of seeing him raise his ears, let out a high-pitched squeal, and come charging to where the girls held out some special treat for him.

But if Curly was already a pretty hefty "baby," it must mean that in Sedalia it was about time for school to begin. And now, instead of the promised decision about school, Mother was telling Tilli that the judge's wife needed a girl to work for her!

"But—" Tilli started again.

"Well, but what, my frisky little chicken?"

Mother seemed so severe when she talked like that. And Tilli didn't feel at all frisky! She was close to tears. "But what about—school?" she blurted out.

There! She'd finally said it!

"Oh, Tilli!" Mother raised her shoulders, then let them drop. "School? That can wait. It won't be for long, anyway. This lady will be coming home from the hospital and wants you just till she gets stronger. She will pay well, too! Now, with the extra mouth to feed and the money to pay on the new farm, we can use every penny."

Tilli sighed. She couldn't understand at all why two farms were needed. She didn't know, either, why Mother and Father worked so hard and wanted everybody else to do the same—all the time, it seemed.

"Then, when I get through there, can I go to school? Will we be back at the brick house then?"

"That's for your father to decide."

Tilli's hopes sagged.

After several heavy minutes Mother went on. "It's perhaps possible, too, that you could get some school in before that—if the judge's wife agrees."

"How?" Tilli asked, her heart skipping a thump.

"Well, there's a convent school near the judge's house. And when the lady's better, maybe she'll let you go there, part of the time, at least."

Tilli was almost too fluttery to get the question out, but she finally asked, "What's a convent school?"

"Oh, I guess it's just like any other school. But the teachers are nuns, called 'sisters'—very holy ladies. And the children have to behave like angels, I hear."

Tilli gulped. She could never behave like an angel, she knew. Maybe it would be better, after all, to wait till Father decided to move back into the brick house.

But it was really the judge's wife who made the decision concerning school.

"Yes," she declared suddenly one day when the judge was home for lunch. "I think our little Tilli should go to school when it is so close by. Will you make inquiries, Judge, of the good sisters?"

The judge looked out from bushy eyebrows very solemnly at Tilli. "Yes, indeed! Yes, indeed!" He pronounced the words with great seriousness, then turned to his wife. "If you think you can manage . . ."

Tilli held very still, waiting for her response.

"I could spare her while I'm taking my afternoon nap," the lady said pleasantly. "She might be able to learn something even in those few hours each day."

That's how it happened that Tilli began spending part of each afternoon at the convent school.

At first she was frightened by the strangeness. The building was very plain and stood behind a high iron fence. The rooms were very high-ceilinged and gloomy. The children marched in silent, solemn lines into and out of their rooms. There was no talking, or scuffling, or playing of games.

Tilli studied the nuns timidly. They did look what she supposed was holy. They carried themselves very straight. And, oh, how beautiful their faces seemed, surrounded by a pure white frame of stiff cloth! Tilli imagined this must indeed be what angels looked like—with no wings as yet, but with long, flowing robes. She told herself she would have to try very hard to be extra good.

It was not easy. Lessons on the afternoons when she could come had nothing to do with "times-ies" or even pluses and take-away-froms. There was some copying of words, words very long and confusing. Tilli could lose her place in even one word: *catechism, transubstantiation, sacramental, venial, infinite.* . . . Then she would take a deep, worried breath and try writing from the beginning again.

One day the sister who taught her class came to look at

Tilli's copying. She scowled at first. Tilli sat rigid. But then, beside Tilli's rough letters, the teacher wrote each word properly in beautiful, even script.

On some days the whole class was questioned, and the boys and girls chanted back in chorus things Tilli didn't begin to understand. She tried to say the answers right after the others or at least move her mouth as if she were responding. Maybe that would help her learn, she thought.

At other times one boy or girl would be singled out to reply. The sister moved up and down the aisle between the desks, asking questions and pointing with a ruler to the one who was to answer.

Tilli always shook a little, fearing what would happen if she were picked out. She couldn't read the booklet that had the answers. The judge's wife patiently tried to drill Tilli on some of the questions. But the ones Tilli had learned would never be the ones asked in school.

And then one terrible day the sister started coming down the very aisle where Tilli sat! The beautiful white frame still seemed like one fit for an angel's face. But Tilli felt frozen stiff as the teacher drew nearer.

"What is the main attribute of God?" the sister demanded. That close, her voice sounded especially sharp. She glanced at Tilli for one piercing moment, then touched with the ruler the shoulder of the boy who sat right in front of Tilli.

There was silence. The boy shifted in his seat, but still said nothing.

"I asked you," the sister repeated more sternly, "what is the main attribute of God?"

The boy squirmed out of his seat very slowly.

"Well?"

"I—I don't—know," he mumbled. Tilli heard the class suck in their breaths.

"So!" said the teacher, her voice rising, "you don't know! You didn't study the lesson for today!"

Tilli saw the boy's head sink lower and lower.

"Then I will have to tell you. Out with your hands— palms down! And quickly!"

Tilli had never seen it done, but she began to guess what would happen next. She tried to slide down in her seat not to see.

Whack! went the ruler down, Tilli was sure, across the boy's knuckles. Tilli cringed as though they had been her own. Through her body more than her mind flashed times the Baelks back in Europe had punished her.

"So you don't know!" the sister almost shouted. "I have to tell you the answer, do I? God is—"

The whacking sound came again—"love!" And again the sharp crack! "*God is—love!* Now maybe you'll remember!"

Cold horror gripped Tilli.

She couldn't get to the judge's home fast enough that afternoon. Her face still felt taut, and her heart was pounding loudly.

"Do I have to go back to that school anymore?" she asked as soon as she caught her breath.

"Why, no, child," said the judge's wife. "I suppose not. But you were so eager— What's the matter?"

Tilli tried to tell about that afternoon.

During the report the lady turned away. Tilli couldn't see her face. Finally she said very quietly, "You must try not to be upset, Tilli. She probably teaches the way she was taught herself—somewhere in Europe, probably."

That must be what made children back there sometimes afraid of school, Tilli guessed.

"But don't worry," the judge's wife was saying. "I was going to send you back home, anyway, whenever I could get word to your mother. And, my, she'll be proud to hear how much help you've been to me. I'm going to let some of my friends know what a good little worker you are."

That promise didn't make Tilli happy. Mother might ask her to help someone else. And then would there ever be any more regular school?

Chapter 11

Any prospects of more school seemed very far away, once Tilli was back with the family at the farm again. She was soon swallowed up once more into a world of familiar chores, but it was a life entirely different from the one she'd known in Sedalia.

She found herself busy with the others, harvesting beans and shucking corn, gathering the potatoes Albert dug, and milking.

"Hey, not so clumsy!" Albert would complain. "And don't throw them so hard. They'll get bruised, and then I'll get blamed."

Tilli wanted to answer back, "Then do them yourself!" But he would surely report that to Mother or Father. And she could guess he was as unhappy about some things as she was and therefore unusually cross. Just as he had started back to school while working part-time for Mr. Brown, the Sedalia photographer, their parents had brought him back home.

New neighbors, the Wills, angrily claimed Albert had trapped rabbits on their land. When Father tried to laugh off the complaint, they smashed the traps, then tore down a wide stretch of rail fence along the back fields to let their cows into Father's best corn.

"You should have heard Father!" Melia reported to Tilli. "It took Mother to keep him from shooting those cows right then."

"Do that and there'll be no end of trouble!" she had warned.

So Albert was called home to help repair the fence and to husk the trodden corn before the fall rains would ruin it completely. One harvest job led to another, and he was still not back at school.

Father said he couldn't spare time from more "taming" of the creek, which he wanted to do so that it would flow in a still wider, new curve, safely away from the little house.

If they hurried through their work, Tilli and Melia could sometimes watch him. It was exciting to see how he upended huge boulders from one place and settled them into another.

One hazy fall day the girls took Feodor along. But he soon grew tired of staying still and wanted to toddle off.

"Don't let him get out of your sight!" Tilli ordered Melia. "I'll go let Curly out of the pen so he can come hunt acorns on the hill."

"Why don't you watch Feodor?" Melia retorted. "You needn't be so bossy, just because you get to go to school more than I do. I can get Curly just as well as you."

"Oh," Tilli agreed, "all right." She hadn't meant to get cross or bossy, just because she'd been thinking about missing school herself. No wonder Melia felt the way she did.

Melia started the familiar call, then went racing to free Curly.

"Come, Feodor," Tilli urged him. "Let's go find some nuts."

He let Tilli lead him up the hill where the big oaks and hickory trees towered above them. The dry leaves rustled under their feet as they shuffled along. They tickled Tilli's toes. Feodor broke into little chuckles as he kicked the leaves ahead of him.

Soon Melia was shouting from the pen, "I've let him out. Call Curly."

Tilli did, and in moments he was bobbing toward her. "Come here, Curly!" she urged him to even greater speed. "See—lots of new acorns."

They all laughed as he began snuffling among the leaves, crunching acorns as he went. He actually looked happy as he crackled each mouthful.

"Let's kick some leaves into a big pile," Tilli suggested. "Then we can roll in it. It'll be fun!"

"Oh, yes!" Melia laughed. "Let's!"

They began spraying leaves in all directions at first, then decided it worked better to scoop leaves up with their hands.

"See here, Feodor," Melia said. "Now we're going to make a big, big pile. Like this—"

Soon he was squatting down, trying to collect leaves in his fat hands. When he had a few, instead of directing them to the pile the others had started, he threw them over his head in a rain of brown and red. He laughed and repeated the fun.

It looked like more fun than just making a pile. Tilli decided to join his game. But by now there were too few leaves heaped on the ground to scoop up easily.

"Let's go where Curly is. There are lots more there," said Tilli.

Soon they all were tossing leaves over their heads. Curly was grunting contentedly between mouthfuls of acorns.

Tilli stood a moment to catch her breath and laugh at him. Near her Feodor began reaching for a handful of leaves, then stopped. "Da!—Da!" he gurgled and pointed ahead of him.

"What, Feodor?" Tilli asked. "What is it?" Then she saw, and her skin began to creep.

Not two yards in front of Feodor, the leaves were stirring strangely. In spaces between them, Tilli caught glimpses of a reddish brown, scaly rope weaving along. Then from under the collection of leaves nearest Feodor, a nearly golden triangular head was thrust out, tongue flicking.

A copperhead! How often Father and Mother had warned of such a snake! But here was the real creature, and Tilli seemed nailed to the spot.

Feodor reached out his hand farther. "Da!—Da!"

Tilli's spell broke. "Back, Feodor! Back!" At the same instant she reached over to pull him toward her.

But before she even touched his hand, there was a kind of delighted squeal, a sudden rush, a brief scuffle. And there was Curly, chomping down on the copperhead. Its tail and head were still squirming as they disappeared down Curly's mouth. He looked even happier than over the acorns.

Tilli was shaking and dry-mouthed as they all hurried home. She was careful that their route was over the barest stretches of ground they could find.

When Mother heard what had happened, she threw her hands up to her eyes, then sank into the nearest chair. "God in heaven!" she exclaimed between short breaths. "I never would have thought I'd be thanking the dear Lord for that runty pig!" Then she rushed over to Feodor and wrapped him in her arms. "My boy! My boy!"

Not many days afterward, Mother made an astonishing announcement: "Next Sunday we are going to church. We have been ungrateful heathens long enough."

Tilli's heart danced. She had never been to church that she could remember, and she wasn't sure her parents had. But she had seen several of the Sedalia churches. The judge and his wife and the Hoffmans always dressed in especially nice clothes on Sundays, when they went off to services. They came back smiling and talking about a "good sermon" or the people they had met. Often Mrs. Hoffman would sing parts of church songs. Tilli thought them beautiful. Church must be wonderful, something like school.

"But how can we go?" she asked Mother.

Mother almost snorted. She sat up very straight. "We have a team of horses now, and our own wagon, haven't we?"

That wasn't what Tilli meant. She wondered about clothes for such a fine occasion. Mother had her black picture dress, and Father his good suit. But what about us? Tilli worried.

She soon discovered that Mother must have planned for everything. She was home all the rest of the week. And what a busy time that was! Dresses were washed and carefully ironed, shirts starched, shoes rubbed till they were shiny. Mother brushed Tilli's and Melia's hair every day. She finished a new wool jacket for Feodor from a blouse she had been given.

By the time they were expecting Father and Albert to

come in from hitching the team to the wagon, the girls were about ready to go. Their faces were scrubbed and their eyes sparkly with anticipation. Tilli's heart was pumping loudly under her clean dress as Mother tied a cotton ribbon in her hair.

Then the door flew open. Father and Albert stood staring inside. Tilli could tell by Father's wild look that something was terribly wrong.

"What is it, Anton?" Mother asked, drawing in her breath.

The question was like the turn of a lock. Father let loose some of his most violent expressions. Finally he got down to facts.

"That bedeviled four-legged fool! Gets caught in the barbed wire! And now she's got a cut on her leg long as my arm!"

Mother's hand flew to her mouth. "That screech owl last night! I knew something would happen! It always means bad luck."

Tilli remembered other times, too, when Mother had talked of strange omens. It was frightening to have Mother be disturbed that way. Tilli felt goose bumps rising all along her arms.

"You'll have to help hold her, Vina," Father was saying. "And, Albert, get me the coal oil and some gunnysacks to wrap around the cut. We'll be lucky if her blood doesn't get poisoned!"

Mother slipped into the bedroom. Before Tilli had time to wonder what Father's bad news might mean, Mother was back—in her ragged farm work clothes instead of the beautiful black dress.

She paused for a glance at Tilli, who was clutching Melia's hand, cold as her own.

"Take off your ribbons, girls." Mother's voice was flat and toneless. "And your shoes . . . Feodor's jacket, too. And say the prayers you know. That's all the church we are going to have."

Tilli looked up, her spirits sinking. Tears were running down Mother's cheeks as she turned and trudged out the door behind Father.

Tilli thought something inside her was about to burst, she felt so tight. It was only the second time she had ever seen Mother cry.

There was no talk of church after that, though the horse quickly recovered. Father sometimes read from the old German Bible he kept under the eaves, but those days grew farther apart. There was no more said about school, either, for what seemed a very long time.

Finally there was the day when Mother came home with the news that she had another "place" for Tilli.

"She's a fine lady, Mrs. Gilpin. Strong, too. But with a new baby, she thinks she'd like help," explained Mother. "And from what I hear, she can easily afford it."

Tilli was aflutter with questions, but she kept listening.

"And the house! Wait till you see it! Nicer than the Hoffmans'."

Tilli was eager to ask about something much more important to her. But Mother was ahead of her. "And listen to this, my girl. As soon as she gets on her feet again, she will let you go to school along with her two boys."

A happy shout was about to break from Tilli's throat when she stopped herself. What if that was the convent school? "Where?" she asked cautiously. "What school?"

"Why, the school where you went those other years. Where else?"

Tilli almost danced. She did clap her hands.

"I'm going! I'm going to school again!" she sang out, to nobody in particular.

Chapter 12

Things turned out even better than Tilli had hoped.

Yes, the Gilpin house was really splendid, with one bedroom just for the two boys, another for their mother and father, and even a dainty, fairylike nursery for the new baby.

And Tilli! She had a room all to herself, a little niche off the kitchen downstairs. There were frilly white curtains at the windows and hanging from a half-circle high over the head of her soft, smooth bed. It was like a princess's room, Tilli was sure. At first she made the rounds, touching the flouncy curtains, the fluffy pillow, the shiny wood footboard of the bed.

And yes, Mrs. Gilpin was a fine lady. After a few days, she was up most of the time, showing Tilli gently just how she wanted the beds made, the glowing furniture dusted, or Baby Jim covered.

Before long she was having Tilli work with her in the kitchen, not just rinsing or wiping dishes or taking scraps out to Fluffy, the yellow kitten. Mrs. Gilpin let Tilli help in making bread, showing her how to soften the hard, cornbready yeast blocks, to sift the flour for her, and, after Mrs. Gilpin had the dough kneaded to a plump ball and put into the big bread-raiser, to check it from time to time to see when it had grown to twice its first size.

Best of all was watching Mrs. Gilpin make the loaves.

"Here, Tilli," she'd say. "Would you like to make a loaf for just yourself?"

Would she! Of course Tilli would answer with a happy, "Oh, my, yes!"

Then the lady would squeeze off a little ball of dough, show Tilli how to flour her hands and, on a small space on the bread board, roll the dough to a tiny long shape. Then she could put it into the special one of the pans she'd greased—just the right size for Tilli's little loaf. It was such fun really making things!

And at last there was the thrill of seeing her very own little loaf taken out of the pan to cool. When she ate some of it with sweet jam or freshly churned butter, Tilli decided it tasted even better than any of Mrs. Gilpin's big loaves.

If the bread was, oh, so good, the lady's pies and cakes were even more luscious. Such eating they made! And sometimes when she made them, too, Mrs. Gilpin let Tilli try making little ones for her very own so that she could learn.

The lady would always smile when she talked to Tilli. "You're going to be a fine cook someday," she once told Tilli. "You learn so fast."

Tilli felt herself standing straighter. Mrs. Gilpin must really like her, and she seemed to want to teach her so many things.

Only they weren't school things! And Tilli kept wondering about what Mother had mentioned.

At last one day Tilli got up her courage to ask Mrs. Gilpin about school.

"Yes, yes," she answered pleasantly, "soon as I can make some proper dresses for my little girl."

The way she said that puzzled Tilli. She thought she should protest that she was Mother's girl—and Father's. But just the same, she felt warm and especially nice inside.

And that mention of dresses? She looked down at her dull gray one made over from some of the old clothes from the farm cabin loft.

"I have this," she said, to be perfectly truthful, even while prickles of curiosity stirred her. "I wore it lots to school last year."

Mrs. Gilpin put an arm around Tilli and drew her close. "Just wait a bit till we get some more diapers and receiving blankets hemmed for Baby Jim. Then we'll start some things to make those blue eyes of yours shine the way they should."

Tilli wasn't sure she wanted to learn about hand-stitching blanket hems. But if that had to be done before she could go back to school, she would do her best. Mrs. Gilpin had many needles, but Tilli didn't lose or break any of them. She did prick her fingers many times and almost bit her tongue off while she concentrated on trying not to make her stitches as big as crow's tracks. It was tedious work, and she often grew impatient to be finished.

At last Mrs. Gilpin began the first dress for Tilli. It was such a pretty blue-and-white-checked piece of cloth! Tilli watched closely every stage of the making and helped where she could. Mrs. Gilpin explained what was happening at each step, and why.

"We have to keep these edges even and the checks matched while I cut," she'd say. "So hold it here, and put pins in along here." Or, "Pull this thread tight like this, to make the gathers. Here, I'll show you."

Each step was more interesting than the last. Little by little Tilli could guess what part of a dress some piece of cloth would turn out to be and how the whole would look when finished. But she wasn't always sure. It was a bit like a puzzle.

Then came the morning when Mrs. Gilpin held up to her the dress, all done! Tilli couldn't believe that what she saw was so.

"I finished it last night as a surprise, my little girl," Mrs. Gilpin said, smiling. "Shall we try it on?"

Well! Tilli was breathing so fast, she couldn't answer. There before her was a dress from a happy dream, flouncy, pretty, blue as a chicory bloom!

It took only a flash for her to be stepping out of the scratchy Mother Hubbard and reaching for the new dress.

Even as Mrs. Gilpin slipped it over her head, Tilli had a whiff of the magic smell of the new cloth. She was prancing with eagerness as the dress settled down on her shoulders and Mrs. Gilpin began buttoning her up.

"Hold still, will you, little Miss Flibbety-gibbety!" she half scolded. But a laugh rippled her words like the gentle chuckle of water over the stones in Flat Creek. "Now, let's see how you look."

"How do I?" Tilli asked, her heart dancing as she stepped back for the lady to see.

"Just the way my little girl should."

Tilli looked down. She took in a big breath. All around her was blue-and-white froth—ruffles edged with lace—two rows of them!

"Oh, my!" she gasped. "Oh, my, just look! It's even much nicer than what the other girls at school wore."

Mrs. Gilpin's eyes had happy crinkles about them. "Well, this is just a start. You'll need several more, and some decent underthings."

Tilli hardly heard. "Now can I start school again?"

"Yes, my dear. I've already talked to Miss Jones. You're to begin next week. The boys will show you where to go."

It was the same public school but a different room, of course, and a different teacher. Some of the same children from her class of last year were in her room. Tilli thought they seemed glad to see her. And with her new dress—! Why, she was like the rest of the girls!

But by now they had gone far ahead of her in their lessons. Again she had to strain to understand what was happening and what she was expected to do.

She worked as hard as she knew how because it was so good to be back. Miss Jones was patient with mistakes, and she suggested which things Tilli should study most.

After dismissal Tilli always raced back to the Gilpin house. When she was through helping with Baby Jim or the cleaning or getting the potatoes ready for supper, there might still be time to practice reading or writing or saying the "times-ies."

Billy and Joe, the baby's older brothers, often listened to Tilli as she struggled with words from her reader. They thought it great fun when Tilli made a mistake. But they always laughingly helped her say the words correctly in the end.

And no matter how hard she tried, Tilli made many mistakes. Some letters always confused her, like the difference between *g* and *j*. If she happened to say *jo* for *go,* or *gay* for *jay,* the boys nearly turned somersaults as they rolled about on the carpet, laughing, just as if Tilli had said the funniest thing in the world.

"Well, which is *gee* and which *jay?*" she asked in desperation. "I just can't keep them straight."

And the boys roared in delight. Or they rocked their chairs while they chanted, "Jabba-gee, jabba-jay! How can she say it right? Jabba-gee, jabba-jay!" On and on.

Finally Tilli would turn upon them. "Oh, you! Who's a jay? And who's maybe a—parrot?"

She couldn't really be annoyed with them, though. They were lovable boys. And to herself she promised, "When I finish the year I'll know the difference, for sure! Just wait and see!"

Sometimes their mother herself stopped the teasing with a gentle "Now, boys, that's enough. Come, Tilli, I've something to show you."

And there would be the start of a wonderful surprise— another dress or a frilly petticoat or perky bonnet!

From time to time Mother or Father would stop by at the house, to bring the Gilpins cabbages or potatoes. Then Tilli could show off her new things.

Sometimes Melia was along. Then what a lot of catching up Tilli had to do! And how timidly Melia would feel the laces on the new dresses!

When her sister fingered the ruffles that way, Tilli felt very strange. It was the same as when Mitzi looked so enviously at Tilli's first new dress back in Europe.

Tilli couldn't help noticing the holes getting bigger in Melia's plain, made-over dress, or thinking of the two sisters in an old folk song Mother and Father often sang.

Those sisters were the daughters of a "Markgraf on the

Rhine." Both married happily but lived far apart. Sad to say, the younger one was widowed early. Without support, she then sought out the castle of her sister. But she went disguised and hired out as a servant in the sister's household. The one year she intended to serve turned into seven.

At the end of that time, she became ill and was at the point of death—from overwork, Tilli was sure. Since she was no longer useful, the mistress of the castle asked concerning her family so that she could be sent home. Only then did the younger sister reveal who she really was.

Then how shocked and sad the older one was!

> *"Ach nein, ach nein, das kann nicht sein*
> *Dass du bist mein verloren' Schwesterlein! "*

> *"Oh, no! Oh, no! It cannot be*
> *That you're my long-lost sister-kin!"*

Father and Mother always sang the many, many stanzas lustily, but Tilli could scarcely hold back tears at those words. It seemed to her the saddest thing possible that only too late would the truth become known. That happened when family heirlooms were shown from the servant-sister's old chest and she confessed:

> *"My father was Markgraf on the Rhine;*
> *My mother, the high king's daughter fine."*

Tilli would be sobbing quietly whenever she heard the very last part, when the dying sister refused the tardy offer of fine garments:

*"I need no silks and satins now:
I need only a little shroud."*

Of course, Tilli knew it wasn't her fault that she had fine clothes and Melia did not. "I never made her work hard at home," Tilli argued with herself. But still she was troubled and couldn't get the song out of her thinking whenever Melia visited.

She always hurried to offer her sister, "Want to try this dress on? I'll help you."

Of course it would be too long and too big. But Melia's eyes went wide as she looked down at the swirly skirt. Tilli promised herself that it would be Melia's as soon as she grew to fit it.

And when Mother stopped to see Tilli, she said with a twinkle in her eyes, *"Ja,* you are a fine little lady now— right? Maybe you would like to stay in this 'castle' all the time?"

Tilli's thoughts flew to school, her pretty room, the ruffly dresses. "Oh, yes!" She said it so fast she didn't give herself time to think how Mother would feel. In another second she was sorry she had been so quick. She glanced at Mother.

"Well," Mother was continuing without a change of expression, "from what she says, your Mrs. Gilpin would like that, too. She wants to adopt you, Tilli." Mother paused and looked strangely at Tilli. "What would you say to that?"

Was Mother serious? Or was she teasing in the puzzling way she sometimes did?

"Adopt? What's adopt?" Tilli asked.

"Why, she'd make you—like her own daughter." Mother stopped to swallow. Then she became gruff. "With nothing but boy children, I'm not surprised. She'd like to have you here all the time."

How that idea set Tilli's thoughts popping about!

From that time on, she felt like on a teeter-totter, now up, now down. When she wore one of the wonderful dresses, she imagined how nice it would be always to live with the Gilpin family. When she thought of being away forever from Baby Feodor and Mother and Father and Albert—and Melia!—everything inside her went tight and cold.

Something seemed very wrong about that. Then there would be the little breads or pies, or Mrs. Gilpin's soft voice giving her lessons in sewing, and the wonder of being in school—and Tilli would think this the happiest life ever. To be always warm and clean, and pretty . . .

"Are you really going to adopt me?" she asked Mrs. Gilpin one day.

That lady looked at her strangely for a moment. Then she spoke very quietly, her arm around Tilli. "I'd like to, Tilli. And your mother hasn't quite said no. I think she understands about the things we could give you here." Mrs. Gilpin sighed. "But, of course, I don't see how she could ever give up such a good, dear child."

Tilli wriggled uncomfortably.

"Would you like to be my little daughter? We all love you here. You must know that."

It was good to hear, but still Tilli didn't know just what to say. "I guess so. . . . Yes, I guess I'd like it. It's all—you all are so nice here."

Tilli knew that was very true. But there was something else—something important missing.

"Would my sister Melia still be my sister here? Would she be adopted, too?"

Mrs. Gilpin was silent a moment. Then she said gently, "Well, no—that wasn't exactly in my plans. I couldn't think of taking you both from your mother, could I? You see, then she wouldn't have any little daughter. And that wouldn't be fair, would it?"

No, Tilli couldn't imagine what Mother would do without Melia as well. But not to have Melia, her own sister, her very dearest, closest friend, as a sister anymore! Tilli choked up starting to picture what that would be like. And no Mother again . . .

Yet to leave this house, her special room, kind Mrs. Gilpin, Billy and Joe—all she enjoyed here—and school! That seemed almost as hard. What could she do or say?

"Couldn't I just keep doing what I am?" she ventured, and then hurriedly wiped her eyes with one fist.

"Of course, of course," said Mrs. Gilpin, patting her soothingly. "You're to stay here till school is out, anyway. Your mother promised that."

Chapter 13

When Melia next visited Tilli, they spent a very long time together in Tilli's room. There were more new clothes to show and many things to tell about what had gone on at school.

But Melia didn't brighten at Tilli's reports. She just looked glum. "I don't think I'll ever be going to school again." She sighed.

"Oh, of course you will, Melia. Soon's you're a little older, you can do like me here."

Melia shook her head slowly. "No," she answered. "Mother says she needs me at home. It never stops! There's always so much to do, Tilli! And I get so tired, always working."

Tilli almost said that she got tired, too. But she knew it was different here from the continual farm work.

Suddenly Melia's face brightened. "But, you know what?"

"What?"

"I already can milk Bossy, just like you!" She illustrated with the necessary motions. "Only"—and she sighed again—"my bare feet get so cold on the ground when it's still frozen like now."

Before Tilli could say anything, Melia was giggling. "But if she's down on the straw before I start, then I put my feet next to her. It tickles, but she gets me warm that way."

Tilli couldn't even smile back. She glanced down at the pink ruffles of her newest dress to the shiny real-leather shoes Mrs. Gilpin had bought her.

"It won't be too long, Melia," she promised, "and I'll be done here. Then I can help you."

"Mother keeps talking about that time," said Melia. "She says as soon as the lady makes you the clothes she promised, and school is out, you'll be home for good."

Tilli was puzzled. "But I thought—" she began, then checked herself. She couldn't really tell her sister about maybe being adopted. "But," she started over, "not till school is out?"

"I guess so." Melia took a deep breath. "You're so lucky, Tilli! You know, I haven't gone at all this year."

"Oh," Tilli said brightly, "just you wait till I finish this year. I'll teach you everything I've learned. You still have your slate?"

Melia shrugged. "Parts of it. Feodor broke it, but I was supposed to be watching him. So it's my fault, really."

"That's all right, Melia. You can use mine." How she wanted to cheer her sister up! But Melia's face was set on gloom. Tilli tried another question. "How is little Feodor behaving?"

Melia shrugged. "Oh, he gets into all kinds of mischief, as usual. Goes where he's not supposed to—like by the barn lot, where he got the barbed wire stuck in his hand."

Tilli sucked in her breath as if it had been her own hand that was hurt. "Oh, Melia!"

"Father had to cut it out. Tilli, it was just awful. I tell you, I couldn't look—the blood and all. And Feodor crying so!"

Things were churning sickeningly inside Tilli. "Is it still bad?—bleeding and all?"

"Oh, no, no, not now. It's all better. And he's right back to being a regular wiggle-hans, into everything! It'd take a dozen people to keep track of him. And, Tilli . . ." She leaned close and whispered, "Know what?"

"What?"

"I think—I just *think* there's going to be another baby."

Tilli's mouth opened wide. "Why?"

"Well, it's just that Mother's so—" Melia motioned with her hands. "And she has to rest so much."

"Oh!" was all Tilli could say. Would Mother again be worrying about "another mouth to feed"?

"I'm only guessing, Tilli," Melia went on. "I don't know. And anyway, that's not all I could tell you about Mother."

"What else?"

"Well, Tilli, just be glad you weren't home—I guess it was Thursday."

"Why, what about Thursday?"

"Oh, some men came to the farm. In a fancy buggy they were. Father was away. So they started shouting at Mother."

"Shouting? What about?"

"I don't know. It sounded like something about money."

"What money?"

"I told you, I don't know! After a while they went to the new barn, you know. And they started to put bridles on the horses, Tilli! They were going to take our horses away!"

Tilli couldn't speak. She knew how proud Mother and Father were to have their own team.

"That was when Mother— Tilli, you won't believe me. But it's true, cross my heart and hope to die!"

"Of course I'll believe you! But what happened?"

"Well, she lifted one of the rails from the fence there— really! And she started after those men, just as if they were flies she was going to swat." Melia paused for a new breath.

"Don't stop!" Tilli begged. "Then what?"

"I was too scared to look. But I still heard her shouting."

"Mother shouting! Shouting what?" Tilli couldn't imagine that. Sometimes Mother and Father argued, and Father shouted. But when she was angry, Mother would just say something sharp in a low voice and draw her mouth tight.

"I don't remember what all, Tilli. But it was terrible. She was like Father, when he's excited, you know how— worse, maybe."

"But tell me what she said! You must remember something."

"Well, she used a lot of awful words—and something about how they couldn't take our—livelihood, I believe it was. It sounded like that. And about something being the stock law. She said they'd better leave quicker than the snakes they were, or she'd—" Melia stopped.

"She'd what? Go on!" Tilli wanted to shake her sister to hurry her story along.

"I shut my ears. I don't know what else she said. But I guess she kept going after them with the fence rail. I told you I was afraid even to look. But when I did, the men were in the buggy again, clattering down the lane. They went so fast they kept scraping the wheels against Father's rock fence there—you know."

"With the horses? Did they take our horses?"

"No!" Melia said proudly. "Without our horses—just the ones on their buggy."

Tilli took a gulp of air and let it out again. "Oh, my! I'll bet Mother was mighty glad then."

"Well, she didn't look glad at all. Her face was all red. And she was breathing so hard, I thought she would die right then."

A chill shook Tilli. She suddenly remembered that it was Father alone who had brought Melia this time. What if Mother—? Tilli couldn't finish the thought. "But she wasn't—? She didn't—?"

"No, she got all right again after a while. But I was so scared to see her that way!" Melia clutched at Tilli. "I tell you, I never was so scared before. Oh, Tilli, if only you'd be home with me again!"

For a long while after Melia was gone, Tilli felt numb. There just didn't seem any happy way things could go for her from here on. She wanted to help her family to be well and happy. What if something terrible like what happened to Victor made every day heavy and sad again? But how she wanted to stay in school and maybe stay here, too, for a long time!

That night she went about her room, slowly feeling everything within reach—the smooth bed, the curtains, her chair, her books. She kept seeing Melia's worried face as she had clung to her. Again Tilli pressed her pink dress close to stare down at her leather shoes. How happy she had been when Mrs. Gilpin had bought them! And now—!

It would be the "big people" who would decide about her being adopted. Anyway, it would still be many days before

Tilli might be going home to stay. Both Melia and Mrs. Gilpin had said that.

But now, as she tiptoed about her room, Tilli felt she was really saying good-bye to all the wonderful things in this place and to her almost-family.

An ache spread deeper inside her with each careful touch. How she would miss everything at this house! She guessed that Mrs. Gilpin would miss her, too. Would Billy and Joe be sorry not to have her as a sister? If she somehow stayed, would they always be fun as brothers, or grow to be like some of the big boys at school?

Why, big boys included Albert, her own older brother! Only now she recalled hearing about the family where he had stayed in Europe. Usually she didn't listen much when Albert talked about them. But she remembered hearing that they didn't want him to go.

What if they had adopted him? How would she and Melia ever have reached Mother and Father and home without him? Maybe Tilli would still be at the Baelks'!

How bossy Albert seemed on that long trip from the Old Country! But what if he hadn't been along? He knew all about where they were to go. He had the leftover money and the important papers. He always watched out for them, showing them things, and keeping them safe from going where they weren't permitted or could get hurt.

And now what a big tease he could be! But, like Melia, he was missing out on school because Mother and Father needed help with the farm work. Tilli knew very well that he would much rather be reading books at school or helping Mr. Brown at his photography shop.

It seemed Tilli would never get to sleep that night. She kept turning from one side to the other. So much was whirling through her head! Unreleased sobs kept her throat tight. Tears that wouldn't break out, yet made her eyes sting and her nose stuffy. Things she wanted to keep forever in her world seemed to be drifting farther and farther off. And she couldn't do anything about it.

She lay quiet for a while, holding Lotti close, watching the moonlight turn the curtains into lacy clouds and dream ships that could carry her into another world.

"Never mind," she finally promised herself, blinking in the half-dark. "Just wait!" It was the way she had tried to comfort Melia. "Someday—just wait and see! I'm going to have a wonderful house with a room like this, all pretty and warm. . . . And my baby will have a cozy crib, and get a bath almost every day. . . . And there'll be red portieres in the doorway to a big, big dining room. . . . And—what else? Oh, yes, and a telephone—one that really works. . . ."

The deep ache and the tightness were slowly easing.

"And I . . . oh, I'll make little breads and pies with my girls. I already know how, almost. And . . . I'll always talk softly, just like Mrs. Gilpin and Miss Jones . . . and look like Mother when she wears her beautiful picture dress. And I'll never keep my children home from school for *any, any* reason at all! And they'll all have nice clothes to wear. . . ."

Tilli yawned and turned once more. She was awake enough to tumble back into the present. But she let the dreaming go on.

"And, soon's I'm home, I'll help mind Feodor . . . and make little toys for him, from walnut shells, the way we used to do for ourselves. Or I could stuff another squirrel skin. . . ."

Even now she smiled into her pillow, remembering the

joke she and Melia had played on Albert. If only he hadn't stayed angry about it! "Oh, yes, Feodor—I could tell him stories from my reader, when he gets bigger, and show him the pictures—maybe even those in Father's Bible, if Father'll let me. . . .

"Mother? Of course, for Mother I'll do lots of the work so she doesn't get too tired . . . and help her get ready so she can go to church whenever she wants . . . or take care of the new baby—if there really is one. . . ."

Tilli moved Lotti away from the pillow, but stroked the matted hair. She thought of how Melia's hair shone when Mother got everyone ready for church that time. Tilli pictured how she would comb and brush her sister's hair and fix it to look that way always. Oh, and sometime she would make her a dress like one of her own new ones. She had watched Mrs. Gilpin almost enough to know how, she thought.

Tilli felt happily drowsier at each dreamy promise. The big, cold ache had been melting in the warm plans for her new world. She smiled to think how pretty Melia would look in a blue dress—no, maybe a pink one would be nicer. . . .

And, oh, much more important! Tilli would explain to Melia everything she had learned in school—the hard "times-ies," the *gee*'s and *jay*'s, if she could keep them straight herself! They would play school together, only for real. And of course Tilli would have to be teacher and make Melia do everything just right.

Only at recess they'd be children, sisters again, playing games together—Rock the Sameron as round we go, counting off with "Intry, mintry . . ."

They would have all kinds of deep secrets to share and

plans to make. Oh, they would have such good times and laugh a lot together!

They would . . .

Tilli's daydreams merged into sleep-time dreaming.

Chapter 14

Once school was over, Tilli had little chance to daydream of the years ahead. Father came the very next morning, and they were soon jouncing in the wagon along the rutted roads out to the farm.

Tilli only half heard his orders to the team or his enthusiasm for crops yet to be planted. She was still remembering the way Miss Jones had said good-bye.

"You've done so well, Tilli, for the time you were here. Of course, I know how things are with your parents. But if only there were a law making school compulsory for young children!"

Tilli didn't understand, but she felt good just the same.

"Do try to be back next fall!" Miss Jones urged her. "I have the next grade, too. And I shouldn't be surprised to see you take some prizes there—if you can just attend regularly. Wait!" she continued as Tilli moved to leave. From her top desk drawer Miss Jones took out a small box. It was one that held those tiny paper gold stars given to pupils who got perfect marks. Miss Jones picked out one. "Let's have your reader," she said.

Puzzled, Tilli fumbled to hand it over.

Then, right inside the front cover, Miss Jones pasted the gold star! "For trying so hard, Tilli!" she said, smiling.

Now on Father's wagon, Tilli kept peeking to be sure the star was really there. She could hardly believe it.

And Tilli thought of Mrs. Gilpin, folding the pretty dresses into a box for Father to take to the waiting wagon. Tilli wanted so much to say something. But she didn't know quite how to begin.

"I wish—" she started, then had to stop and give a hurried jab to her eyes. "I don't know what I wish— It's been so nice here—"

"Don't feel bad, my dear," said Mrs. Gilpin. "I wish things, too, that don't always happen as I might like. Everybody does."

Surely not somebody like Mrs. Gilpin, Tilli thought.

Mrs. Gilpin was continuing in her gentle way. "We mustn't let disappointments hurt too much, Tilli. Sometimes we may just be reaching for the wrong star—when there are lots of others."

She must have sensed how that puzzled Tilli. For she asked with a half-smile, "You don't understand, do you?"

Tilli shook her head slowly. Did she mean the gold star?

"Well, never mind, my dear. Just remember how glad I am that you had the chance to go to school and to wear these. And you must know we've all been so happy having you with us."

Now, as she was riding home, Tilli could still feel thrilled but sad, too, over Mrs. Gilpin's last warm hug.

"Yes," Father was saying, "we have everything ready for the bean planting. The ground is wonderful this year. And wait till you see how I've piled the stones where the creek was trying to gobble up our land!"

So it went all the way to the farm.

Melia was the first to see them coming. She raced to meet the wagon as fast as her bare feet could pick out a way on the rough, stony road.

"Melia!" Tilli shouted before she jumped down.

There were happy sparkles in Melia's eyes as she began spilling out the home news. Tilli quickly shoved thoughts of Miss Jones and Mrs. Gilpin aside. She was with her own dear sister again!

Even before she went into the house, she had to see Melia's very own little garden with its short, wavy rows of lettuce and beets. And even before she started sharing school news, Tilli was listening to how Melia had fixed up the little cave near the biggest oak tree into a tiny playhouse.

Mother gave Tilli a quick, eager squeeze. "Well, my little wanderer, it's good you're here. So much to do, and I—" She spread her arms wide and sank into a chair.

She did look tired and heavy. Tilli was eager to carry out the promises she'd made back at the Gilpin home. But before she could think where to start, Mother took charge. "Better change right away," she directed. "Albert has the beans ready to put in now."

That was about how things went for Tilli that early summer. Something was always blocking the fine plans she'd made.

Of course, the planting and hoeing and weeding did help Mother in a way. Tilli often got very tired herself. But that didn't seem to stop Mother from getting tired, too, and sometimes cross.

And of course Tilli played with Feodor, but he didn't always want to do what she suggested. Of course, too, she tried to teach Melia the things she had learned at school. But to do that, Tilli had to take the part of teacher, and Melia complained that she was being too bossy. Often it was just more fun to play at the cave "house," when they had time.

What happened was often very different from what she had so glowingly planned.

But there was at least one wonderful event she couldn't have planned at all.

It happened on that strange morning when Mother stayed in bed instead of going out to work in the fields.

After gathering the wood chips for the kitchen stove that day, Tilli and Melia came inside to find a queer smell about the bedroom, and Mother in her nightclothes hastily mopping up the rough boards. On the bed was something pink and squirming.

"Oh! A baby?" the sisters squealed. "Can we see?"

"Not just now, girls," Mother answered, her voice strained and faint. "Yes, it's a new little sister for you."

Tilli saw how Mother staggered toward the bed. Then she turned and spoke more softly than ever before, yet with a teasing half-smile. "Let's see, now—which one of you would like to have her for your very own, special sister?"

Both girls shouted, "Oh, me!"

"Well," Mother said slowly, "I haven't yet done the milking this morning. So—whoever milks the cow—"

Tilli didn't wait to hear the rest. She ran for the milk pail and dashed outside.

When, with Melia close at her heels, she returned with the foamy milk, Mother was lying in bed, very thin and tired-looking. But beside her she held the sweetest little baby ever.

"And she's mine!" Tilli told herself, her chest swelling with proud happiness. She saw the blush of color on the baby's cheeks. "She's like a rose," she said excitedly. "I could call her Rosie—couldn't I?"

And that became the baby's name.

Certainly from that time on, watching over "her very own" Rosie was ever so much more wonderful than playing with Lotti had been. Surely no other baby ever had such round, little sausagelike toes, such chubby legs almost always pumping at the air! And such funny, adorable little goo's and gurgles came from the tiny mouth! Why, "her" very special sister was more lovable than even Feodor or Baby Jim.

Tilli thought that from the very beginning the baby knew its name and smiled whenever Tilli whispered, "Hello there, my Rosie Dumpling!" Mother said it was too young to understand, but Tilli was sure she knew better.

How she hated to leave Rosie to go out to the fields for the summer work! But there were other times when she could spend a whole afternoon talking or singing to the baby—or an evening watching her asleep in the log cradle.

"Guten Abend, gute Nacht," Tilli would sing, as she had heard Mother do:

> *"Lullaby and good night.*
> *With roses o'er spread,*
> *With angels to guard*
> *Is Baby's wee bed.*
> *If God wills, thou shalt wake*
> *When the morning doth break. . . ."*

Or Tilli would change the lines of another cradle song:

"*Sleep, Rosie, sleep.*
Your father tends the sheep.
Your sister shakes the dreamland tree
And drops a little dream for thee.
Sleep, Rosie, sleep."

Sometimes, with Melia helping, Tilli used one of the school songs, "Ring Around a Rosy," "London Bridge," or "Go in and out the Window." Once or twice they forgot themselves and exploded loudly on "Pop Goes the Weasel." Then Rosie stirred and opened her eyes for a flicker, but soon relaxed into quiet sleep again.

More than ever before, Tilli disliked having to spend time in town when Mother arranged for her to help people. It was never again the Gilpins, but always some others with a child or extra housework for "just a few days." Those days might stretch out to be a week or more.

Tilli was afraid. What if Rosie forgot her in the meantime? But when home again, Tilli felt smile-y all the way to her toes as the dimpled face would turn her way after she called, "Hello, there, my little Rosie!"

After almost each absence, however short, Rosie could do something new. Maybe it was watching her own plump fingers weaving in front of her deep-blue baby eyes. Or maybe it was trying to flip over. When that finally happened, Tilli was even more excited than Rosie herself.

Before very long, the baby started creeping forward on the big bed, in little bumping moves. She looked so like an inchworm looping over a log that Tilli had to laugh.

"Look!" she called to Mother. "Rosie's crawling!"

"*Ja,*" Mother warned, "now you'll have to watch her

closer than ever. That one will be getting into trouble. So quick she is when she wants to be! Soon it'll be one wink you see her, another wink, she's gone."

"Not with me," Tilli told herself. She'd certainly always be able to keep ahead of such a little tot.

Thoughts of Rosie kept Tilli so busy she hardly realized it when the time came for school to begin again.

"I've got you another good place," Mother exclaimed one morning. "It'll be about like for Mrs. Hoffman. This lady needs someone for a month or more."

Tilli's heart suddenly felt heavy. To be away from Rosie that long!

"And listen to this, Tilli," Mother continued. "She'll let you go to school every day, except washdays, that is."

School again! Tilli clapped her hand over her mouth to hide her surprised grin. In the next second, though, thinking of Rosie, she wasn't quite so happy.

But at school that first day Miss Jones was all smiles. "Oh, you did come back!" she greeted Tilli brightly. "I'm so glad!"

And when Tilli peeked into the reader for that year, with more beautiful pictures than her last one, all the old rapture returned. Here she was, really and truly! And starting with the rest of the class!

At the very start she was often able to fling her hand up first when Miss Jones asked the class a question. She was even one of the early ones chosen in the first ciphering match of the year. It was such a wonderful feeling to belong, to be able to keep up with the others!

"Class," Miss Jones announced one day, "I want to tell you about the prizes we'll be giving this year."

Tilli listened carefully as Miss Jones mentioned the usual spelling and general excellence awards. But how could she hope to compete for those?

"And new this year," Miss Jones continued, "will be a special prize—this set of three books." She held each up in turn. "One is about geography, one is on history, and this is a storybook—see? Now, who will get this prize?" She waited while the room became very still. Tilli hardly breathed. To have such books!

"The pupil who makes the most progress in all studies during the term." Did Miss Jones look directly at Tilli? It seemed so. Then she went on to urge everyone to try his very best.

But Tilli hardly heard. Her mind was jumping ahead. She could almost imagine having those books for her very own. Oh, to be able to study their marvelous pictures, figure out their wonderful facts, read the stories! And to win, she needn't be best, like Harry there or Sarah. The winner would just have to be much better than now. In other years Tilli had promised herself that and made the promises come true in most ways. She surely could do that again, if she just tried hard enough.

Then she remembered, and her hopes began to sink. She was probably going to be here, for sure, only a few more weeks. She remembered, too, about Rosie back home. Again she worried. Was Rosie being watched over carefully enough?

Oh, how that worry was misplaced! So that Rosie would be safely cared for, Mother took her along when she herself began again to work for other people, this time far off in a place called Kansas City.

But little Feodor!

How many times afterward Tilli prayed that she could blot out that dreadful time when Father stopped where Tilli was working to say she must come home with him.

"Why?" Tilli asked, then right off wished she hadn't.

Father, often so jolly, looked stricken. He talked like someone who had been stunned.

"I think you might want to see your little brother before we bury him," he stammered, turning his face away.

Feodor? Bury him? Lively, bubbly little Feodor? Tilli felt a stab of cold fear.

"Why? What's happened?"

"Later," Father mumbled. "Get your things—and hurry. The lady says it's all right for you to go. She can get along now without you."

Tilli collected her books and her few clothes in a bumbling daze. Half-thoughts of the school prize, of Father's face, of fear of what she was still to hear, all were spinning into a blur. She couldn't think.

On the long trip home, she learned the awful story. Between deep sighs, choking sobs, and occasional blasts at himself for not having been home, Father told it to her.

He had been cutting wood at the other farm. Mother was helping out a Kansas City friend of one of her "ladies." The others were home, the older ones with orders to dig the potatoes.

Tilli grew sicker with each detail: about the October chill, the bonfire where Feodor had been left to stay warm, his getting too close to the flames, and his screams, which the others heard too late to save him.

If only she had been home, Tilli thought, it might have been different. But she couldn't be sure. And how could she have endured to see the child suffer or hear his last, lisping call for water? Just trying to imagine those terrible things turned her world black.

Many times in the Old Country Tilli had thought she had reasons to be very sad. Now she was sure it would be easier if something worse happened to her than to someone like her dear little brother.

How she tried to block from memory those dreadful days that followed—things she had seen, things Father and Mother had said and done. After a while Mother scarcely said anything. She seemed not to notice that she had any living children left. It was as if nothing mattered to her anymore.

And if Mother had none of her old sparkle, how could Tilli feel anything but strange and miserable? But having Melia to share the distress helped. The sisters grew even closer than before. Scraps that had sometimes risen between them were forgotten. Tilli tried hard not to deserve being called bossy. Melia was more careful with Tilli's books and slate pencil. They both found some comfort in being extra loving and careful with Rosie when she was home. Even doing some hard chore without being told helped some.

But deep inside, Tilli had a hard knot of fear that wouldn't leave. Would terrible things always happen to their family—just when it seemed all was well?

Sometimes when the shrunken family was gathered quietly sorting the beans or picking out the nutmeats, a sudden fear would seize Tilli. Then she would slowly realize she was peering from one to the other, wondering . . . Long ago there was the half-remembered little brother in the awesome white box. Then it was poor Victor . . . and Feodor. . . . Which one of them would be next?

Once upon a time she had counted out things she hoped

for from being in America: enough to eat, the chance to be in school, a real family of her own around her.

Well, she hadn't been really hungry for ever so long. She sensed dully that the hope for more school had died with Feodor. But she worried about something that she now realized was much more important to her.

Could her dear family ever be safe from trouble or be happy again?

Chapter 15

Then, just like dancing sunlight after a long, dark rain, Father came home from Sedalia one day, his formerly solemn face all a-sparkle.

"Look, Vina!" he called to Mother, holding out a queer-looking crinkled, nearly round box. "A concertina again! And I haven't forgotten how to play one—after all these years!"

He pushed his wrists through handles at each end and moved his arms apart. A wheeze of sound came out. Tilli stared, her mouth open. In another instant Father was squeezing the box shut, then pulling it out. Parts of merry tunes flowed out when he tapped his fingers on little buttons at each end. What a marvelous box, Tilli thought.

But Mother's face clouded. "For shame, Anton!" she snapped. "With our little Feodor scarcely in his grave! What could you be thinking?"

Father stopped his playing. But twinkles were still in his eyes. "Well," he admitted, "to tell the truth, I was thinking that I might never get another bargain like this, that's what. The poor fellow—he must be a greener greenhorn than I!—needed more money to get to where his countrymen are in Kansas. This was all he had left to sell.

See?" Father played more music to demonstrate. "It's still in good shape."

Mother continued to scowl. "And where did you get the money?" she demanded.

"Oh, I had that sack of beans, and—"

"Anton!" Mother scolded. "That was to help pay the interest."

Tilli was confused by the talk of beans and interest. She didn't want to think about the man who had to sell his magical box, either. She wanted to hear Father play some more.

"But, Vina," Father was protesting, "now I have a concertina again! Look how nice it is." He reached it over in Mother's direction. "Now our singing will really sing!"

"But, Anton! Sing? . . . when our Feodor . . . " Mother wailed.

"Yes, Feodor . . ." Father began quietly, brushing one free hand across his eyes. "Don't we always pray that he himself is now singing with the angels? Isn't it time we think of the other children, too, Vina? We still have a fine family left."

Mother said nothing. Her shoulders were shaking as she stared at her hands.

Father turned to Tilli. "Isn't that right, my girl?"

Tilli couldn't answer, but she straightened up. So Father was still proud of them all!

"But Feodor—" Mother was continuing.

"Now, Vina," Father said, more tenderly than Tilli had ever before heard him talk, "no one should grieve forever. How does the Holy Book say? 'Weeping may last for the night, but gladness comes with the morning.' "

He freed one hand and laid it on Mother's quaking shoulders. Tilli held her own stiff until Mother quieted and Father stepped back.

He started fingering the buttons again. "Besides," he went on more briskly, "surely you remember there are all kinds of songs. And how many times have we already found the saying true, 'Sorrow shared is sorrow eased'?"

For the first time Mother raised her head to nod solemnly. Then she dropped it again. *"Ja, ja."*

"Remember this one?" Father tapped out a tender melody. Then, moving the box more boldly, he sang:

"Ich habe den Frühling gesehen . . ."

"I have seen the greening springtime,
I have greeted all the flowers,
Harkened to the nightingale,
And kissed a lovely maid."

Before he got to the second stanza, Mother had joined him in a phrase or two, tears glinting in her eyes.

"The lovely spring is now wasted,
The roses are all past their bloom,
The nightingale's song has been silenced,
And my loved one is deep in the grave.

"Spring's loveliness will come again,
The flowers bloom anew,
The nightingale find voice once more,
But my dear one will never awake."

It was a song new to Tilli. As she listened, her throat seemed to swell shut.

When the song was finished, Father stopped and nodded his head. *"Ja,"* he said with a deep sigh, "that says it all for us. It helps to remember others have suffered, too."

"Ja, ja," Mother repeated, "it helps."

Next they both sang another melancholy tune, "How Is It You Are So Sad?" Their faces still looked sorrowful, but more at peace than they had in a long time. Tilli's own tautness was easing. She felt exhausted, as though she had been crying for hours.

Father was making several starts on a song Tilli recognized as one she had heard in Sedalia. Finally he made it swing the way he wanted. Tilli figured it was about a cowboy who had died in a fight. The words were gloomy, but Father sang them with gusto:

"Oh, beat the drums slowly and play the fifes lowly!
Oh, play the Dead March as you carry me 'long.
Take me to the graveyard and turn the sod o'er me,
For I'm a young cowboy, and I know I've done wrong."

Father had to stop in the middle of the next stanza. *"Ach!* I can't remember the rest."

"No matter," Mother said gruffly. "They are not worth remembering, anyhow. There are better ones from the Old Country."

"Ja, ja," Father nodded. Soon he was playing and singing one Tilli knew only too well—a poignant tale about an innkeeper's lovely maiden, now lying on her bier.

When her parents began the song about the Markgraf's daughters, the one that always made her choke up, Tilli couldn't stay in the same room any longer. Father and Mother were wrapped up in their singing and even smiling at each other. But Tilli slipped hurriedly to where Rosie was sleeping, and quietly shut the door.

Watching that peaceful face slowly lifted the heaviness inside her. And after a long time she was aware that the singing in the next room was very different. The concertina's music was louder, and she guessed the thumping she heard was Father stomping out the catchy rhythms. She found her own feet tapping the floor.

Even through the closed door Tilli could hear some words: "Hi lee, hi lo, hi lee, hi lo! With us it is always the longer, the poorer . . ." But the tune was lively and jolly.

When she finally stole into that room again, Tilli noticed Mother was lightly clapping her hands and singing lustily, too.

"Fine, Anton!" she exclaimed when they finished one song, "You're good as ever! Now, what else—? You still remember '*In Lauterbach*'? You know . . ." She began singing as she clapped, " '*hab ich mein' Strumpf verloren. . . .*"

"*Ja,* sure!" Father laughed, squeezing out a swinging rhythm to join her.

To Tilli it sounded very silly. Some man was joking over losing his leggings to pay for drinks. But Father and Mother were making it seem a marvelous adventure.

Then followed dance-y tunes of many kinds. Some had words, some none, when Father played and pranced about at the same time. Before long Albert and Melia crept into the room, big, surprised smiles rounding their faces. Tilli smiled back at them. Everyone joined in on the foot-tapping or clapping.

After that first time, Father often played his concertina.

The others would turn either sorrowful or lighthearted, depending on the tune. Sometimes it was one of the lullabies Tilli liked to sing to Rosie. They went so much better with the music from his wonderful box.

It was exciting to Tilli to learn many of the sprightly songs. But she still liked best those with a sweet-sad melody or story. Most of those reminded her keenly of little Feodor. But she tried not to let her thinking show. Mother seemed more like her old self now. What if she should again be always sad and silent?

Of course, marvelous as they were, the new songs couldn't completely break the spell of grief or ever bring back the happy times before Feodor died. They couldn't always release that deep fear she had, or quite fill the hollow that came when she thought of all the lessons her school class was having. In spite of trying to forget, the old wishing always sneaked back.

Once, for a few short moments, it looked as though that wishing would come true again.

"Rosie is getting just too much for me to have along with me in town," Mother said one day. "The ladies don't like it if I have to pay too much attention to her. And nowadays someone has to be watching her every minute."

"Oh!" Tilli's heart took an extra strong thump. Her mind was racing ahead. "Then you'll be home with her? And I'll be going back to Sedalia—and school?"

"Not so fast, my girl," Mother said. "You are to keep her here, and I'll work for the ladies. I can make more money than you."

Tilli looked down at her own toes.

"You think that you and Melia can take care of her by yourselves?"

Tilli nodded meekly. "Oh, sure," she said. Still, she had to gulp back tears.

She loved watching over her little Rosie. But why, she wanted to ask, did she so often have to choose between two happy things? Miss Jones's wonderful prize was surely no longer possible. There was still school, though, and just thinking about it made Tilli feel very sorry for herself. Not to be able to do one of the things she liked best!

"Now, now," Mother said, patting her shoulder, "missing school is not the end of the world, *Mädchen!*"

How did Mother know what was going through Tilli's mind!

"Try to think of your own mother and father—and your fine Mrs. Gilpin."

Mrs. Gilpin! Tilli hadn't thought about her for a long while. "Mrs. Gilpin?" she asked. "What about Mrs. Gilpin?"

"Why," Mother began, drawing Tilli close, "do you know what she once told me?"

"What?" Tilli asked.

"Well, she said she liked to help you because she didn't have the same chance as you."

Tilli listened in disbelief. She had always thought that everybody in America except herself could do as he wished.

"It seems," Mother went on, "that when she was a little girl, she had to teach herself. Her parents couldn't read— not so well even as I, I guess—though they owned a few books somehow. And there weren't any schools at all around where they settled—out in Kansas Territory, it was then.

"Hmmm. . . ." Mother mused, more to herself than to Tilli. "Now I think of it, that's about where we'd have settled if that flood the train ran into hadn't scared some of us back this far. . . ."

Tilli's mouth had been opening, but she was too astonished to say anything. Mrs. Gilpin—who spoke so nicely, and who knew just about everything! She had taught herself—hadn't gone to school at all? Did that have anything to do with what she'd said about "other stars"?

For a while after Feodor's death Tilli had tried to find comfort in her small pile of books. But nothing then had seemed very important. What good were the books if she'd never go back to school?

Now she was beginning to feel ashamed. What would Mrs. Gilpin have thought of her, had she known?

"Do you really suppose," she asked Mother in a very small voice, "I could do the same as she did?"

"Well," Mother answered briskly, "how do you think I—or your father—learned? As the saying goes, 'Only to the bird that never tries is flying impossible.' If you're as smart and as spunky as I think you are . . ." She left the rest unsaid.

Tilli straightened up. She remembered the happy verse about the little bird so eager to fly. Well, she promised herself, I can keep trying!

Oh, how she tried! Whenever there were free moments, she went over her "times-ies" alone or with Melia. She reviewed the stories in her old readers until she could not only say almost all of them by heart but also spell nearly every word in them. And she worked especially on the stories in her new book.

Sometimes Albert even let her look at his last reader, too. She studied it hard, figuring out, letter by letter, the new, longer words until they made sense to her. Sometimes they didn't at all, and she became discouraged. But usually, if she kept at it, she could read even long, strange words!

It was true, then! Like Mother and Father—and Mrs. Gilpin!—she could keep right on learning, by herself, even without a teacher! That way, nothing could really hold her back, ever! Whatever happened, she could keep learning— all her life, even!

The discovery set up happy tingles inside her. Only— sometimes she still thought of those prize books. How special it would have been to have them. . . .

Once in a while Father brought home a sheet of the Sedalia *Bazoo*. If she begged, he would let Tilli watch while he read aloud ever so slowly the English he still had trouble pronouncing. She followed where his finger pointed, and generally could help him say the words correctly.

"That's my Tilli!" he'd exclaim. "If she says so, then it must be right. She always tells the truth."

That made her very proud. She could help even Father! Usually it was Albert who did that.

Father didn't read very often, though. By summertime he was generally gone, sometimes taking Mother and Albert with him for work elsewhere. Tilli and Melia were then left to manage chores and to care for Rosie alone.

Little Rosie had indeed become what Mother called "a handful." She was beginning to toddle, and so needed both to be cleaned up oftener and to be guarded more closely.

"Watch out for that quick one!" Mother warned whenever she left the child in the sisters' care. "She slips out of sight faster than a green lizard!"

"I know, I know!" Tilli would mutter to herself after

such advice. "As if I don't! But to call my darling Rosie a lizard!"

"And see that one of you is always with her," Mother usually went on.

"Yes, yes," Melia would reply, "we know."

"Not so cocksure, my fine one!" Mother scolded. "There are plenty of things you don't know." She pointed a wagging finger at Melia, then turned to Tilli. "I'm counting on you, Tilli, to watch out for Rosie. You're the big girl, remember. And see that the chores get done in time."

Tilli would shift impatiently from one bare foot to another and wanted to say (but never felt quite saucy enough), "Well, of course, I'd much rather be with Rosie all the time than doing the old chores!"

Chapter 16

"Tilli!"

Something about Melia's call made Tilli go cold.

"Tilli!" This time her sister's voice was even more insistent. "Rosie's in the well!"

Tilli dropped the wooden spoon into the cornmeal mush she was stirring. Before her mind really registered the news, the desperate scream came again. "Tilli, can't you hear? She's drowning!"

In an instant the cold shock thawed, and Tilli was flying through the kitchen door, then kneeling beside Melia at the cistern's edge, straining to see against the lowering sun and the dark below the well's rim. Her thinking was still paces behind.

"How could it happen, Melia? Wasn't she with you—the way Mother said?"

Melia's grip made Tilli wince. "I—I left the cover off, just for a second, Tilli," she blurted out, "when I came for another pail of water for Bossy. Oh, Tilli, what will Mother say?"

Tilli peered into the dim light of the hole. Yes, down in the water was all she could make out of her baby sister, her own Rosie Dumpling—a mass of whitish dress and thrashing arms.

"What will Mother say!" Melia chanted between ever louder sobs. "Oh, what will Mother say?"

Tilli didn't dare think of that. "Stop it!" she scolded, then called down, "Rosie, baby, Rosie Dumpling, keep splashing! You hear? Keep splashing!"

Tilli began throwing back the rest of the boards covering the cistern. "Run for the ladder, Melia!"

Melia shot off like a rabbit, then suddenly whirled back. "I can't! Father's got it at the other farm, remember?—for the early haying." She began whimpering, "Oh, what'll we do, Tilli?"

Now it was Tilli who hesitated. She stared fearfully into the brick-ribbed hole. "We'll just have to go down without the ladder."

Melia brightened. "I know!—the way I get down the rocks by the creek to our 'house'! Let me, Tilli! I'm faster."

She was already proving that by tossing off her gray Mother Hubbard and, in her shredded underwear, backing down into the opening. "Hang on to my hands, till I get over the edge."

Into the chinks between the wet bricks Melia curled her toes and began inching down.

Tilli breathed hard. In fascinated terror she watched her sister's arms and legs straddle the rough cylinder and move spiderlike down from ledge to ledge. "Oh, Em, be careful!" she warned. "What if—?" She couldn't finish.

From the hollow Melia's voice quaked strangely. "Is she still there, Tilli? I can't look down."

"Yes, I just saw an arm. Only hurry! Rosie Dumpling, keep splashing! We're coming! Melia'll be there!"

But from the dark water Tilli could see no baby smile back. Melia's spider moves blocked all but a churning arm and leg from view.

"Hurry, Melia! Em!" Tilli urged one second, even while she knew that couldn't help, and the next, when she saw Melia's toe seem to lose a hold, "Oh, be careful! You'll fall, too!"

"I'm all right," Melia puffed.

"Try if you can reach her now," Tilli begged. Her own voice reverberating in the hollow seemed as unreal as the happenings now were.

Melia began shoving her feet in tighter and reaching down with a freed hand. Tilli held her breath, then shrieked, "She's gone! She's gone under!" The bobbing white bundle was blurred over by water. "No, there she is again! Grab her, Melia! Grab quick—right there!"

And with a sweep of her arm Melia did grab part of the soggy dress and swing the bundle inside it onto her own shoulder. She looked up to see where to move next.

Tillie let out a deep breath like a quick prayer of thanks. Then she called down, "Oh, Melia, just don't let go! I'm coming to get her."

"No, no!" Melia panted. "There's no room. I'll get her up a ways farther. You reach her from the top."

Tilli lay over the edge of the cistern and tried to stretch down. It was still too far. Then she tried again, by twining her feet around a firm log on the cover and letting her arms and body down over the rim as far as she could. Reach as she might, it wasn't enough.

"Hurry, Melia!" Straining as she was, she could hardly get breath enough for more than a whisper.

Melia squirmed a notch higher, and Tilli could just touch the baby's clammy shoulder. Another shift, and Tilli gasped, "I've got her!"

How did she manage to pull the soaked lump out of the dreadful hole? Tilli hardly knew. Her arms and legs worked almost without direction.

Safely over the edge, she dared to look at Rosie's face. It was gray and still. Only a strip of her rolled-back eyes showed between the matted lashes. The once bright lips were almost black.

Even in the warm summer twilight, Tilli was shaking as if in an icy rain. She laid the limp form on the grass. Rosie's legs twitched, then were quiet.

Melia soon scrambled over to see, too.

"Is she dead?" she whispered hoarsely, then began sobbing. She jabbed her fists to her eyes until her face was smudged with dirt. "She's dead, isn't she?"

"Don't say it!" Tilli barked at Melia. "Don't you dare!" But Tilli could hardly swallow down her own fright.

Rosie lay like a rain-drenched doll. The once bouncy curls were plastered across her colorless forehead.

"Rosie! Dumpling!" Tilli tried to call the child gently from this strange quiet. "My little Rosie!" She started to push the hair away from the baby's eyes and to stroke them. But she pulled back before they were completely closed— the skin was oddly stiff.

Melia reached over to shake the little shoulders. "Rosie, wake up! Rosie, can you hear me? It's Melia."

But the baby didn't stir.

"She's drowned, Tilli! She's—dead! Oh, now what will Mother—?"

Tilli swallowed harder. "I must not," she told herself, "I must not believe it!" But something very heavy pressed at her chest, and she moved jerkily.

She felt Rosie's fat hands. They were cold. She touched the little chubby toes she always loved to brush. They were wet and icy and crinkled like a dried potato.

What could she do? She remembered when she herself had almost drowned at the other farm. She'd been so wet and cold!

"Let's put her in some other clothes, some dry ones, Melia. She's so cold." It was all she could think of to do. Maybe if she had gone to school longer, she would know how to help Rosie now, but— She carried the baby into the house.

"Shouldn't we get some grown-ups to help?" Melia stammered.

"Where?" Tilli turned on her sister so fiercely that the girl burst into new tears. The more she tried to punch down her own fears, the crosser Tilli became. "It's almost dark now, and—and—anyway, who is there? The Wills would never help us. And if you really cared about what Mother says, you'd remember what she said about leaving Rosie alone!"

"I know, Tilli," Melia blubbered. "But maybe the Siddon boys? They're not so far. I could wade the creek if I took off my dress again. Maybe I could."

"No, I said!" Tilli cried out. "No, you can't! Mother said never— Anyway, they're not home. They're just like Mother and Father, helping with haying over in Morgan County."

Tilli really didn't know just how far that was. But no one

she knew ever walked there. "We just can't leave Rosie!" Tilli felt the heavy lump rising again. "Oh!" she lashed out sharply, "why can't you go get some dry clothes, the way I said?"

Oh, why, she thought, when Melia finally started looking in the chest, why did everything go so clumsily? She tried to dry the wet rag doll that once was the lively, lovable Rosie Dumpling. But no sooner would she roll her over and finish one side, than more water would run out from ears or nose or mouth. And Tilli'd have to start over again. With Melia's help she had to turn the floppy bundle over and over to get the dry clothes on.

It was already so dusky inside that more than once they nearly stumbled over a stool or a log near the stove as they went for more dry wiping rags or clothes.

"Let's put her on the bed," Melia finally sighed. "We haven't had any supper yet."

"Melia! Amelia!" Tilli found herself using Father's way when he was severe. "Who wants supper now?" she almost screamed.

Melia turned her face appealingly to her sister. Even in the half-dark Tilli saw the daubed tears glinting. She softened her voice. "Of course you're hungry. The mush is on the stove."

Melia didn't move. Tilli laid the baby down carefully. Its arms flopped on the rough ticking over the corn husks. Tilli could hardly bear to turn away. "No," she decided, "Mother would carry her. I remember . . ."

What did she remember? Something from that first year at home: Mother, gaunt and silent, pacing the floor. She was carrying little Victor, patting his back gently. But he had never awakened anymore. He had been put away in a box Father and Albert had made. And the box was put into the ground and covered over.

No, he would never come back, Tilli knew. Like dear little Feodor, his spirit was somewhere with the dear Lord. Still, Mother had carried Victor when there was something very wrong with him. Tilli knew she mustn't leave little Rosie alone in this trouble. She would carry her, too.

Again she swung the limp form into the familiar position over her shoulder and began patting the body slumped there. Occasionally there was the feel of water trickling down her own back—or was it sweat from her fright? She couldn't tell.

Melia was now huddled on the stoop. "It's getting so dark!" she wailed. "Can't we light a lamp?"

Tilli wanted to huddle with her. But it would never do to let her sister know how afraid she was. Hadn't Mother often said that at almost twelve a girl was big enough not to be afraid?

"We mustn't!" she answered. "Remember Mother told us three things for times she's gone: never leave Rosie alone, never cross the creek, and never light a lamp. The stove, yes, but not a lamp."

For a flash of time Tilli was back at the Baelk home in Europe, remembering a dreadful whipping. Before those people came back from work, she had tried to start a fire in the open grate. They needed a fire to prepare supper, and she had thought to be helpful. But they had been fiercely angry. The punishment had seemed so unjust.

Now, at almost the very instant that Tilli began to understand, there was a new surge of tears from the doorway. Melia sobbed for them both. "That's because of Feodor!"

What could Tilli say to comfort her? She shuddered at the memory of what had happened to him and why. She shifted her burden again. Her shoulder was so hot and tired!

"Oh, what will Mother say to us, now!" Melia wailed again.

What had Mother said that one time, after Feodor died? Tilli still felt a bit odd about Mother because of that. She remembered only too well, because it seemed so peculiar and shocking. Mother had picked up this very same little Rosie when she happened to be crying, and had shaken her, hard. "If it had been a crybaby like this one, instead! But my precious boy, my Feodor!"

As if to protect her now, Tilli held the baby close and rocked her gently, though there was no need to quiet her. How could Mother have been so harsh? Tilli wondered once more.

Then, for the first time, she at least partly understood. Had she not herself, just now, struck out at Melia about supper? And why? For no reason except that she was so terribly unhappy!

Tilli shuffled to the door. With her free hand she reached down to touch Melia's shoulder.

"Melia," she said, "I think the fire's out, but the mush may still be a little warm. Have some for your supper. I left the milk on the table when I strained it."

"I can't see in the dark," Melia protested.

Tilli reached down to take her hand. "We can feel our way. Come. . . . Here's the kettle—and the spoon. Get a dish over there. The milk's here . . . and the molasses."

Melia followed directions, but then began sniffling again. "I can't, Tilli," she complained. "It won't go down."

"I think I know," said Tilli. "There's a kind of thick lump right above your tummy, isn't there?"

"How did you know?"

"I feel that way, too, Melia. Here, try some milk at least. You always like it before it's been in the cellar to cool."

"So did—Rosie!" Melia choked on the name. But she did swallow some of the milk. Finally she sighed a big sigh. "I'm so tired, Tilli. I'll just rest on the bed a little. Then I'll help you."

Soon Tilli heard the corn husks rustle as her sister lay down. Before long there were deep, hard breathings, and then quiet, easy sleep sounds.

And Tilli was alone with her drowned baby sister. From the dark the immensity of her trouble slowly crept upon her. Now she too wondered about what Mother would say.

To think she, Tilli, thought she didn't need Mother's cautions and had secretly felt she might have saved Feodor! Now, look what had happened! To make things more terrible, she was partly to blame.

For a frightened moment she considered running away. Yes, even from the family she had been so happy to find and to love! But in the next minute she changed her mind. How could she even think of leaving Rosie, her own very special sister?

She fought off imagining having to put the baby's body into the ground, like those of Victor and of Feodor. She dared not try to think what it would be like without the soft, warm, cuddly Dumpling.

She attempted all the more to show her love by cooing to Rosie and holding her as tenderly as she knew how. She tried a lullaby—"Sleep, Rosie, sleep—" But her voice cracked. She rocked Rosie and laid her over her knees and patted her back gently again and again. In her weariness she half believed the child was warm and responsive once more.

How, oh, how could she make that come true? What else could she do? What else, besides carrying him, had Mother done with Baby Victor? Then Tilli remembered. Mother had prayed. She had called on the dear Lord, as the unusual tears rolled down her cheeks.

So Tilli prayed—little, short, earnest prayers, with parts of lines recalled from the times Father read from the Holy Book. She tried to repeat the words of that little prayer from her baby days in Europe. How did they go?

"Liebes Kind, Gott der Vater sieht und weiss alle Dinge." Dear Child, God the Father sees and knows all things.

She said them over and over. Once she almost smiled, recalling how she used to think that *"sieht und weiss"* meant *"süss und weiss"*—"sweet and white"—and described God or the angels. But that made her newly afraid.

"Oh, dear God the Father," she begged in choking whispers, "don't let Rosie be an angel yet!"

And always she paced the floor. By now she had memorized exactly where the logs and the stools were, and she wove her way around them. Through the open doorway she felt the fullness of the dark night. There were a dozen strange shapes and a thousand night noises. The katydids close by and the bullfrogs from the creek seemed to be talking about her: "Tilli did it, Tilli did it, Tilli did it!" "Rosie's drowned, drowned, drowned!" "Tilli did it, Tilli did it!"

"Only I didn't do it!" she thought. "I was doing what I was supposed to do, and Melia was to watch—"

But she knew that wasn't good enough. As Mother had said, she was the big girl. Melia was only nine.

"Only," she tried again, "I wouldn't for the world let anything hurt my Rosie." She could feel the curls were dry and bouncy now. "If only—! Oh, my darling Rosie!" Tilli's whisper was almost as hoarse as the frogs' croaking.

My Rosie! How proud she'd always been of that! Now in the dark she tried to picture again this room on that morning when Rosie was born. With each detail—the first sight of the new baby, Mother's promise about the milking, Tilli's winning from Melia, the naming of Rosie—Tilli felt more desolate.

How happy she had been to have her very special little sister! But now—!

"Oh, *lieber Gott,* Dear Lord . . . our daily bread . . . in heaven . . . please don't let her be an angel now, no matter how beautiful!"

With a hot stab of shame and guilt, Tilli remembered how she had once almost been willing to live always with the Gilpins—so that she could have pretty clothes and could go to school.

Oh, how unimportant all that seemed to her now, compared with the joy of seeing little Rosie smile at her. If only that could be again!

Tilli sobbed silently. Yes, she liked pretty things. And she had loved school more than anything else except her Rosie and her family. Now school seemed like a pleasing, quick-fading dream, something remembered as happening long ago and in a different, glad world. She would—oh, so eagerly!—give up even those memories if only things could be as they had been—just this morning! If only . . .

Sometimes with the baby dangling over her lap, Tilli sat

in the rocker and strayed into crazy nightmare worlds—
Rosie struggling in a river of fire, the mush kettle boiling
larger and larger until the frogs came jumping out and
croaking, "Rosie's drowned, drowned, drowned!"

Then she would rock or walk and pray again and doze
again.

Finally her shoulders became so hot and her arms so tired
that she laid the baby carefully down at the foot of the bed.
Melia was still sprawled at the head as she had first flung
herself.

Tilli drew the rocker close to the edge of the bed so that
she could still reach over and pat the tiny back. Pat . . .
pat . . . "Darling Rosie! . . . Oh, dearest God!—Please,
please!"

And then the dreadful dreams again, the more dreadful
awakenings to remember what happened . . . the dreams
again. . . .

Then suddenly Tilli was awake once more. The world was
changed. It was no longer dark. There were no bullfrogs or
katydids, only the cockcrows for the arriving day.

A soft rosy light was sifting through the door and the east
window. Tilli stretched wearily as she slumped over the
edge of the bed. Then the thrust of reality brought her
upright. All the past night was no bad dream, but a
dreadful truth. There was Rosie lying. . . .

Tilli unfolded herself painfully and forced herself to look
over at the child.

There was a delicate pink on the baby's exposed cheek.

Tilli gulped. For a moment she let herself believe the past
had, after all, been a nightmare.

Then she saw that the rose tint of sunrise was on the dress
and the mattress as well.

"Oh, my Rosie!" Tilli tried to speak, but her voice was like a rough squawk. "Oh, Rosie—Dumpling!"

She reached to pat the bundle once more. It felt warm and soft.

One chubby, limp arm stirred, the curly head turned, and Rosie opened her baby eyes.

Tilli jerked herself erect and stared. She drew in a long breath. It was moments before she dared, half-fearfully, half-hopefully, to lean over for a closer look. Had she only imagined the wonderful sight?

No, it was true! Rosie's eyes had drifted shut again. But she was breathing quietly. Tilli touched one chubby hand. Yes, it was really warm!

"Rosie, little Dumpling," Tilli whispered. It came out hoarse and quaky. "Rosie . . ."

Again the eyes blinked dreamily, then opened wide, and Rosie turned on Tilli her dearest smile.

Before she realized she was doing so, Tilli had picked Rosie up to cuddle and was covering her curly head with kisses. "Oh, Rosie, Rosie! Oh, thank you, dear Lord! Thank you!" she kept repeating.

She stood there, holding Rosie to her heart, while surges of happiness began sweeping away all the dread and weariness of that long, long night.

They had both awakened to a new day and a wonderful new world. And there were the wonderful old things as well—the same Rosie here, Tilli's whole family, her books, yes, even the chores!

"Now," Tilli finally said to Rosie, "let's wake Melia, shall we? And then get some breakfast?"

This account of Tilli's childhood in Missouri during the 1880's is based largely on details as she remembered them and often told them to her own children.

Since such recall can easily be uncertain, the narrative's time sequences may vary from the actual order of the events, just as the people met may not have been as they seemed to Tilli. Except in the case of most family members, names of persons mentioned here have been changed where remembered, or invented where not.

My aunt, the Rosie of this story, lived to be eighty-six and outlived all the other nine children born to that pioneer immigrant family. She always credited Tilli with saving her life, but Tilli in turn insisted that without Melia's brave rescue that could never have happened.

ABOUT THE AUTHOR

"TILLI'S NEW WORLD," author Linda Lehmann reports, "continues my mother's story begun in BETTER THAN A PRINCESS, and it, too, is based on incidents Tilli often related to her own children. Such recollections, some happy, some tragic, held us spellbound then, and later helped us to appreciate the heritage immigrants like Tilli left us all. Certainly she always gave our education high priority in her life."

A Chicago native and former teacher, Mrs. Lehmann with her husband left a busy suburban life several years ago for Colorado mountain "retirement." She stays involved, however, with church, garden club, and senior-citizen projects, with "domesticities," and with such outdoor activities as hiking and swimming. A dabbler in oils and watercolors, she regularly exhibits with a local art group. In addition to writing children's stories, Mrs. Lehmann is occasionally represented in the "Poetry Forum" of the Denver *Post.*

The Lehmanns have two grown sons and are happy grandparents.

#3107